The Wedding Twist

The Wedding Twist

The McCarthy Sisters Series

Elle Douglas

TULE
PUBLISHING

The Wedding Twist
Tule Publishing First Printing, March 2025

Copyright© 2025 Elle Douglas

The Tule Publishing, Inc.

ALL RIGHTS RESERVED

First Publication by Tule Publishing 2025

Cover design by Lee Hyatt Designs

ISBN: 978-1-966593-25-6

Dedication

To my sisters, Andrea (*Anne*-drea) and Danielle, and my sister-in-law Andrea (*On*-drea): What a wonderful gift in life to have built-in best friends.

Prologue

I T'S CANADA DAY, a statutory holiday. Newlyweds Jeannie and Everett McCarthy consider it an auspicious occasion to sign the deed to Jeannie's grandparents' lakefront lodge, a former boarding house for seasonal ski instructors in the small town of Keystone Ridge, nestled in the Rocky Mountains of Alberta. The lakeside property will soon be reborn as the Butterfly Lake Lodge, and Jeannie and Everett have dreams of it being one of Canada's most iconic vacation destinations.

They sit with Jeannie's grandparents at the local diner over fried eggs, bacon, and hot coffee and sign on the dotted line. Duke and Sue Carmichael are bursting with happiness at being able to give their beloved granddaughter, and her new husband, the place that has been their business and home for over forty years.

After breakfast, Jeannie and Everett bid Duke and Sue farewell and drive to their new home overlooking Butterfly Lake. Jeannie is eight months pregnant with their first child, so instead of carrying his wife over the threshold, Everett takes Jeannie's hand, and they walk through the doorway they've passed through so many times, the entrance to the place that's now *theirs*.

In the weeks that follow, they bicker about paint colors and disagree about the nightly rate they'll charge for the lodge's rooms, but every day at one o'clock, they eat lunch together in the kitchen at the windows overlooking the Three Sisters Mountain Range, never tiring of the view, minds whirling with excitement and uncertainty. They sink the small fortune Everett made writing high school science textbooks into making the Butterfly Lake Lodge the perfect vacation spot.

A baby is born. A girl.

The lodge opens, and they receive modest bookings. They take out ads in *Alpine Adventures* and the *Calgary Herald* and this helps a bit, but when the reservation-desk phone quiets down in the offseason, Everett pitches a new nature guide to his publisher to make ends meet. He doesn't want to write about nature anymore—he wants to *be* in nature, but he has a family now.

A second baby is born. Another girl. Another mouth to feed, and without steady income, Jeannie and Everett busy themselves with the lodge's operation while silently wondering if they made the right choice.

Everett strategically plants the gardens so nature's revolving splendor will be on display, whatever the season. Larkspur and geranium in the spring, bluebell and mariposa lily in the summer, and Woods' rose and white gentian blooming into the fall.

Jeannie cooks and bakes no matter how many rooms are booked. There's dessert, even for breakfast, just as seasonal as Everett's gardens. Sticky toffee pudding in the winter, lemon cake in spring, peach cobbler with clotted cream in the summer, and pumpkin scones drizzled with white icing in the fall. Jeannie is a big believer that when you're on vacation, anything goes.

Visitors leave the lodge with happy hearts and full stomachs, but the word of mouth only travels so far, and tourists continue to pass them by in droves on the way to the grander hotels in the area.

On a quiet Monday in early June, a travel-weary couple stops by the lodge's front desk. They're on their way to the famous Keystone Ridge Resort but took a wrong turn.

Everett patiently writes out directions for them, and the man realizes his wife has disappeared to the window in the lodge's restaurant. The man approaches his wife. She turns to him and whispers, "Can't we stay here instead?"

There will be a one-night cancellation penalty from the Keystone, but the man feels the pull as well. They borrow a canoe and paddle through the lake's turquoise waters. They indulge in Jeannie's happy-hour snacks and cocktails. They make the short walk into town to shop and dine at a local restaurant. After making love in their room, they sit on their patio and gaze up at the twinkling stars.

While his wife sleeps, the man does what he promised he won't do on vacation: he writes.

He is a travel writer for *The New York Times*, and he can't help himself. The modest majesty of this place, the pristine beauty...he has to share it with the world.

Two weeks later, the article is published: "A Sparkling Jewel of the Canadian Rockies." It's syndicated by papers around the world. The phone rings. And rings. And rings.

Almost overnight, the Butterfly Lake Lodge is booked a year out.

In the leadup to the 1988 Calgary Winter Olympics, three major hotel chains make aggressive offers on the lodge, but Jeannie and Everett decline. This is their home.

A third baby is born. A girl.

The influx of bookings means they can hire a staff, build additions, upgrade linens and flatware, and install hot tubs outside the walk-out suites.

A fourth baby is about to be born, and for a moment, Everett wishes for a boy...until the doctor hands him another perfect girl and he, once again, feels like the luckiest man in the world. He has four daughters.

Celeste, the eldest, is cautious, obedient, and intuitive.

Elodie, from day one, loves being outdoors and always seems to be covered in dirt.

Ava throws the most adorable temper tantrums, and Jeannie and Everett have to stifle their laughter so as not to enrage her further.

And Quinn, the baby, has no trouble growing under the tidal wave of her family's love.

Years pass, knees are skinned, report cards are proudly stuck to the fridge, staff come and go, many welcomed into the fold of the McCarthy family. Keystone Ridge is alive with tourists.

After graduating from university, Celeste takes over the lodge's front desk, and Jeannie and Everett watch in admiration as she, with her gift for anticipating the needs of others and making them feel special, makes their perfect spot even better.

A grandchild is born. It is, of course, a girl.

Then, the world weighs heavily under a global pandemic, and things are slow even after reopening. The yearly insurance-company inspection shows major repairs are needed on the lodge in the coming years. Years of rolling out dough for morning pastries has caused arthritis in Jeannie's wrists. Everett can't seem to leap out of bed with the same energy as he used to.

Jeannie and Everett are tired.

Over lunch one day in early April, over forty years after opening the Butterfly Lake Lodge, they agree to share the news with their girls.

It's time to sell.

Chapter One

"FOR GOODNESS' SAKE. Just come in," Celeste grumbled after the second round of knocks sounded at the door of the third-floor turret room. She'd been lying on the bed in the lodge's smallest but coziest guest room for the last two hours, but even the heavyweight merino-wool blanket she'd pulled over her head couldn't keep out the intrusion.

Judging by the tentative raps against the door, coupled with the persistence of the knocker, Celeste knew...

A) that it was her youngest sister, Quinn, and

B) better than to ignore her.

As the youngest of the McCarthys, Quinn had spent her whole life showered with attention and wasn't about to be disregarded.

Celeste moved the blanket away from her face and watched as the door to the room opened slowly and Quinn poked her head in, with her mop of short curly brown hair and vintage round glasses framing concerned and teary eyes. "I come bearing poppy-seed loaf," she whispered, holding

6

out a plate of Celeste's favorite dessert and taking a small step inside. Quinn set the plate on the bedside table, then slid a bottle of amber liquid out of the pocket of her wide-leg jeans, showcasing it like a game show host. "And Fireball. Ta-da!"

Despite the pit in her stomach and puffiness of her eyes, Celeste couldn't help but grin. "An odd combination," she said. Odd but thoughtful, as always with Quinn, who was likely feeling just as crummy as she was. Celeste shifted over and patted the mattress next to her.

Quinn plopped down onto the bed beside her, then shimmied over and put her head on Celeste's shoulder. "How long have you been up here for?"

From the queen-sized bed, they had a postcard-perfect view of the fondant-iced crest of the Rocky Mountains against the pale gray late-afternoon sky. The flickering gas fireplace was keeping the room cozy. Celeste really just wanted to be alone, but her little sister was like the human version of a stuffie—soft, innocent and oh-so-snuggleable.

She kissed Quinn on the head and glanced at the clock on the bedside table. "A while."

Quinn propped herself up on her elbow, unscrewed the bottle of cinnamon-flavored whisky and took a swig, then passed it to Celeste. "So, they've told you, I heard. I was last up. And Elodie and Ava each found out last night, over FaceTime."

Now the missed calls from her other sisters the night before made sense. She'd been exhausted after turning over a full house that weekend and had sent the calls to voicemail and passed out by nine o'clock.

"Yup," Celeste said and took a small sip, the alcohol burning her throat as it went down. She coughed and winced. "Ugh. I can't believe we used to drink this stuff."

"Used to?" Quinn said. "Are you forgetting Marilyn and Tyler's wedding?"

"I believe that was Elodie and Ava," Celeste said. The two middle McCarthy sisters had taken full advantage of the open bar on the night of their cousin's wedding this past summer at the lodge, and Celeste had been on Advil and Gatorade duty the next day. Given the phone call she'd received only hours before the wedding from Matt, telling he was breaking things off and wouldn't be coming as her date to the wedding, it was surprising she hadn't been the one nursing a hangover.

"So…" Quinn said. "What do you think?"

"I think they're being ridiculous." *Ridiculous* didn't even sum it up. The idea of her parents selling the Butterfly Lake Lodge after forty-five years, when their health was fine— more than fine, actually; Everett and Jeannie were often cited as the gold standard, #SeniorGoals—was nothing short of shocking.

Hours earlier, right after checkout, they'd closed the door to the inn's office, where Celeste had been looking over their reservations for the upcoming week, and given her the news.

Time to retire. Putting the lodge on the market. They'd had enough anyway, Jeannie had said, waving her hand in the air like it was no big deal, like she was declining dessert after a five-course meal. Like it wasn't going to completely shatter their eldest daughter's life.

Celeste had tried to remind them what keeping the lodge in the family had meant to Jeannie's grandparents, way back when they had gifted the lodge to Jeannie and Everett for their wedding, but her appeal to their heartstrings had been in vain. *There was only one of me*, Jeannie had reminded Celeste. *There are four of you. That makes things a lot trickier.*

Plus it was perfect timing, they'd said. The lodge wasn't in disrepair necessarily, but in the next decade major work would need to be done on the roof and the foundation and new windows were likely needed on the entire south-facing side of the building. It would cost a small fortune to do all the work necessary to keep the place going.

Now not only did Celeste no longer get to keep up the illusion that her parents would be around forever, but the lodge, which she loved and where she'd pictured herself working for the rest of her life, had a very uncertain future without the two people who'd been so instrumental to its success.

Whoever the new owners are will want to keep you on, honey, Jeannie had said.

No one knows this place better than you, Everett had assured her. *We can even make your employment a condition in the sale agreement.*

But Celeste knew better. New ownership meant new ideas, new traditions, new blood. With her dual major in history and comparative literature from the University of Victoria, she had no formal training in helping to run a business. She'd just been lucky enough to be born into one.

For the past ten years, she'd managed all of the Butterfly Lake Lodge's operations, from training and scheduling the cleaning staff, ordering supplies, taking bookings, checking in and touring guests, and problem solving the many different curveballs that came along with running their fourteen-room lodge.

Everett and Jeannie were the faces of the inn—Everett as the resident naturalist who created and maintained their award-winning pollinator gardens and grounds and offered astronomy classes, hikes through the woods, and cross-country skiing expeditions, and Jeannie as the chef, baker, and host extraordinaire who made sure stomachs were happy and faces were smiling. Celeste was behind the front desk and otherwise behind the scenes, making sure the lodge maintained its air of effortless calm while ensuring everything ran like clockwork.

"Why do you think they told us all separately? Are they not only selling but closeted masochists as well?" Quinn asked now.

Celeste sighed, then buried her face into her sister's shoulder. "I don't think they could take a tsunami of four daughters' tears all at once. Pass me that bottle."

Another knock sounded at the door. Celeste and Quinn looked at each other. If it was their mother, she'd have likely been listening outside of the door for the past five minutes. Jeannie was notorious for getting into her girls' business, from grilling their friends who came to dinner or for a movie night when they'd been growing up to reading the diaries they'd kept stuffed under their mattresses and in their underwear drawers (an accusation which Jeannie still denied) to having an often infuriating but usually appreciated sixth sense for what was going on in the minds and lives of her daughters.

If it was Everett, he'd be there to get a game of euchre going or convince them to go for a late-winter hike in the forest behind the lodge. Everett didn't like conflict, so smoothing things over with the girls as quickly as possible and pretending everything was okay would likely be top of mind.

The door creaked open slowly, then stopped. Celeste and Quinn burst out laughing as another much larger bottle of Fireball slowly levitated into the room, held up by a phantom hand. It could only be one of two people.

"Elodie!" Celeste cried, and she sat up as the second oldest of the McCarthy sisters appeared in the doorway. "I thought you were away for another week."

Elodie entered, wearing khakis and a weatherproof down jacket, her long auburn hair pulled back into a ponytail, her big, gold-flecked brown eyes filled with concern. A biology professor at the University of Calgary, Elodie was on sabbatical, researching something about mycorrhizal networks, or what she called in layman's terms "trees talking to each other." She'd been using the lodge as her home base in between expeditions to an area in the boreal forest, where she and her team had a base camp.

Elodie spotted the small bottle of Fireball on the bed between Celeste and Quinn and joined in their laughter. "Great minds," she said and looked around the room. "I was supposed to be gone for another week. But after last night's call, I figured I might be needed elsewhere."

"Do Mom and Dad know you're back?" Quinn said.

"They'll know soon enough. I slipped in through the mudroom. I figured at least one of you would be up here."

The turret room had long been the McCarthy sisters' favorite place to hang out, since it offered the most privacy. It was only ever occupied when the lodge was full. Otherwise if someone booked it, looking for the most affordable option, they would always be surprised with an upgrade to a larger suite, with no additional charge. It had also been a great place for a slumber party in their preteen years despite there only being one bed.

Since it was a Monday evening in late April, a time of year when the lodge was only at capacity on weekends, the turret room was conveniently available for the sisters to commiserate.

Now they were only missing Ava, which wasn't uncommon. Ava was a single mother of an eight-year-old girl, Sam, and worked a demanding job in downtown Calgary as one of the city's top investment bankers. In the last few years, Ava and Sam had only been able to make it to the lodge for Christmas, an important family celebration or wedding, or for the odd weekend when Ava's bosses were themselves on vacation.

"Should we call Ava?" Quinn said and slid her phone out of her pocket. If there was a time they would have loved all being together at the same time, it was now.

"Sure," Celeste said. "I doubt she'll answer, though."

Quinn tapped the phone to connect to their sister on FaceTime, while Elodie tossed her jacket onto one of the camel leather lounge chairs by the fireplace, then plopped down onto the foot of the bed and lay on her back. "Ahh..." she sighed. "A real mattress. Lovely."

After three rings, Ava's face came on the screen, features barely visible in a dark room. "Let me guess—you're all sobbing like babies in the turret room," she said before any of them could get a word in edgewise.

"Wish you were here," Elodie said. "If anyone could talk some sense into Mom and Dad, it would be you."

Ava's no-nonsense approach to life and willingness to speak her mind sometimes got her into trouble but for the most part served her well, not only in her career but in life. She was also sarcastic and had been a holy terror of a teenager when she'd been at her hormonal peak, so when Sam had been born, the whole family had gleefully proclaimed that Ava was going to get what was coming to her, but so far, her daughter was as angelic as they came, without even a hint of her mother's fiery temper or dry sarcasm. The whole family doted on Sam, as their only granddaughter and niece.

"Same," Ava said. "But you know how I feel about the turret room. It's haunted. Remember that knocking we heard last time we stayed there?"

Celeste rolled her eyes at Elodie and Quinn, but they all remembered that ill-advised Halloween Ouija-board sleepover over twenty years ago.

A sharp rapping sounded at the door, and they all screamed. The door flew open, and there was Ava, dressed in a perfectly tailored plaid Smythe suit, her light brown hair in a top-knot bun, and an overnight bag in her hand. "I'll take that," she said, dropping her bag onto the floor and reaching for the Fireball, dodging the pillow Elodie threw at her.

"You scared us, witch," Elodie said, laughing. "Where's Sam?"

"In the kitchen with Mom. That should tie Jeannie up for a while. Let's get into it."

Despite the reason that had brought them there, the four sisters were thrilled to be back together. For the next hour, they dissected their parents' news with a fine-tooth comb, interspersed by jokes, tears, and catching up on the minutiae of their lives.

When a knock came at the door and Jeannie entered with a tray of raspberry white-chocolate scones fresh out of the oven, pretending she hadn't been loitering outside of the door waiting for a break in conversation, they quickly changed the topic to the upcoming wedding the lodge was hosting that weekend, their mom's Pilates classes, the neighborhood gossip—anything but the elephant in the room. Celeste noted that Jeannie looked tired, as though announcing her retirement had given her body permission to age overnight.

"Mom, are you okay?" Quinn said.

"I'm better now," Jeannie said, taking in the sight of her four girls sprawled out across the guest room, eyes shining with the delight of a mother whose nest was full again. "What do you want for dinner? Sam's in the kitchen having some minestrone soup and toast. I've got some nice tuna steaks in the fridge I can marinade for poke bowls. Or if anyone wants gnocchi—"

"Let's just order takeout," Celeste said. If Jeannie cooked, it would be an hours-long affair, and all she really wanted to do was eat dinner, then go to bed.

Everett was down at the rec center for his Monday-night house-league curling and wouldn't be home until late, so after Celeste checked in with the evening desk attendant, they returned to Jeannie and Everett's house behind the lodge. Elodie and Quinn read Sam some stories, then tucked her in while Jeannie ordered Indian takeout.

For their mom's sake—or maybe theirs?—they opened a bottle of Cab Sauv, turned on some reruns of *The Office* and spent the rest of the evening pretending everything was normal.

IN THE MORNING, Celeste sat at the computer in the lodge's office, grinding her teeth and trying not to smash her laptop against the desk. The lodge's new accounting management software, which they'd been forced to migrate to after the former company had gone defunct, was as intuitive as wandering backward through a maze. Part of her short fuse likely had to do with a sleepless night, head spinning with her parents' news, panic mode about the future of her job fully activated. She wasn't trying to make this about her. But it *was* kind of about her, wasn't it?

And now she had to figure this new software out—and fast. Taxes were due at the end of April, and their bookkeeper in town would be expecting everything to be up to date and error free. With the last system, Celeste had known exactly where to plug in numbers in order to keep track of money coming in and going out, even though she'd had no idea how it all ended up getting reconciled. That was what the bookkeeper was for. The new system, however, asked all kinds of questions about percentages going to OTAs and PIE settings and other acronyms, and she couldn't figure out what to do with the damn thing.

"What's wrong?" she heard from over her shoulder. Celeste turned to see Ava in the doorway, wearing her high school track hoodie and a pair of faded jeans. Of course it would be Ava, whose commerce degree had set her up to do this task in her sleep, but through her annoyance, Celeste was glad to see her sister looking casual and relaxed for once.

"Nothing," Celeste said. "When are you heading back to the city?"

"I'll work remotely for the rest of the week," she said. "Sam's basically ahead of everything at school, so I don't mind her being out of class. I think it'll be good for Mom and Dad too. They seem a little…on edge."

"What does Tyler think of that?" Ava's new boyfriend had traveled with her the last few times she and Sam had visited the lodge, although Sam only knew Tyler as Ava's "friend" and nothing more. Tyler was nice enough, but Celeste could tell Ava wasn't all in. Ava was guarded and private; no one even knew who Sam's father was, and anyone who was bold enough to ask promptly had their head bit off.

"He's fine. He's out of town anyway," Ava said, and Celeste detected something in her eyes. "Your cheeks are splotchy," she said, coming to look over Celeste's shoulder. "Something's wrong. Whatcha doing?"

Celeste took a deep breath in. "I'm just inputting some petty-cash purchases. Or at least I'm trying to. This new software is really confusing."

"This is easy. You just…" Ava reached over to point at something on the screen, and Celeste swatted her hand away.

"Maybe easy for you," she said and slumped back in her chair. "We're not all financial-whiz kids."

"It's just simple accounting," her sister insisted. "I can show you."

"You might be able to show me this one thing, but everything else in this program is different. And I have no idea how to use it. Which makes me pretty much useless in my job, and no one is going to want to hire me once this place is gone." Her voice wavered, and she willed herself not to cry.

Ava's expression softened. "It's not gone yet," she said. "And whoever buys this place would be crazy not to keep you on. You know everything about the lodge. And you're so good at your job."

"There are no guarantees," Celeste said. "And there are plenty of people with training who could easily slide into this role."

"You've always been good at math. You can learn this quickly—with some online tutorials or something. Or there's no reason you can't take an online accounting class. All of this will make sense, no problem."

Celeste didn't want to take an online accounting class. She didn't want to learn this dumb new software. She wanted to go back to using Hospitality Hub version 4.3, to when her parents hadn't been selling the lodge, to when she'd still had a job with a future to talk about at her monthly cocktails with friends. Was that too much to ask?

She looked over to see Ava typing on her phone. "Here," Ava said, flashing her screen. "Oakview College offers a course. It starts next week. Every Monday night from six to eight."

Ava read the course description out loud, which had a lot of the language Celeste recognized from the parts of the new program causing her trouble. Oakview College was only a twenty-minute drive south from the lodge, just east of Canmore, and offered courses in everything from woodworking to introductory Spanish to digital marketing. Monday nights were slow at the lodge, so she wouldn't be missed.

"How much?" Celeste said. She didn't love the idea, but Ava might be onto something. Getting a paper credential would be important when she was forced to search for a new job, and in the meantime, there was this stupid petty-cash report that needed reconciling.

"My treat," Ava said, tapping furiously into her phone. A minute later she looked up and grinned. "Confirmation's in your email. Consider it an early birthday present."

"Happy birthday to me," Celeste grumbled.

"I've got to make a couple of calls for work. See you at dinner," Ava said and left Celeste alone in the office.

Her sisters all had their thing: Elodie, her passion for teaching and biology. Ava, her success in the business world. Quinn, her burgeoning social media empire. What did Celeste have? Had she too easily fallen onto the safe-and-accessible path and piggybacked off her parents' success?

She sat in her chair, staring at her laptop. Sitting around and sulking about it wasn't going to help. She'd do the course, update her resume, and keep her eye out for good opportunities.

Some clattering sounded from the kitchen as the intoxicating aroma of apples, butter, and cinnamon floated into the office. Celeste stood up and made her way to the source of the delicious scent.

She might soon be jobless, but in the meantime, there was pie.

Chapter Two

AFTER DISTRIBUTING THE last of the pheasant feathers onto the desks arranged in a semicircle around the classroom projector, Jack Wallace glanced at his watch and guesstimated about fifteen minutes until his students would start trickling in. *His students.* He had to laugh. For many unsuccessful years his parents had encouraged him to go to teacher's college and join what they, and his many aunts and uncles and two brothers who were also teachers, called the "family business," and now he was finally fulfilling their wishes, though maybe not for the reason they'd wanted him to.

He ripped his golf shirt free from the waist of the khaki pants he'd bought earlier that day from Sporting Life and felt a fleeting moment of relief. Jack knew very well there were different classes of outdoorsmen—outdoors*people*, he reminded himself—and that this nook of the world some-times attracted some of the douchier ones, but he didn't care. He knew with 100 percent certainty that he was more experienced than anyone who was about to walk through that door, so whether he was wearing a penguin suit or boxers and a T-shirt, he was in charge of this space.

So why did he feel like he was about to vomit up the Subway sandwich he'd wolfed down on the way over?

He cleared his throat, then picked up a printout of the class list Oakview College had emailed him a week earlier. There were six people signed up for his course in classic fly tying, about six more than he'd anticipated when he'd pitched the course to the college a few months earlier. Six was also the minimum number that he needed to be able to run the class, so he had to knock this intro session out of the park and make sure everyone came back next week.

He passed out the remainder of the materials onto each student desk, then picked up a whiteboard marker to write the agenda for the class on the board, as his mother had suggested in an email with unsolicited classroom-management advice. *Your students will always keep things interesting*, she'd signed off. Whatever that meant.

Why people would register for this course was beyond him. Fly tying was an art form that he'd learned from his grandfather growing up, but there was an instructional video for pretty much everything these days on YouTube. But he wasn't about to complain about the much-needed revenue stream, which would fill in some gaps in what was so far shaping up to be a slower-than-usual spring for his fly-fishing expedition business.

And some people, Jack figured, just wanted to get out and socialize.

He couldn't relate.

A man with a silver ponytail and a blue parka popped his head into the classroom. "B107-A?" the man said. He was in his mid-fifties, bearded, and wearing a T-shirt advertising a local craft brewery, exactly the clientele Jack had expected to attract.

"You got it," Jack said.

"Bryant Harris," the man said.

"Jack Wallace. Welcome." Jack gestured toward the semicircle of desks, each one laid out with the materials they'd need to make their introductory fly, the Silver Blue, a great option for fishing in shallow waters like the nearby Bow River. Over the three classes, he planned to show them the Leadwing Coachman, a Hare's Ear Parachute, maybe a Smokejumper or a Skirrow's Fancy. Depending on the enthusiasm, but mostly the skill level of the group, maybe they'd attempt a Jock Scott for their final class or at the very least he could show the group some samples from his collection.

Shortly after, a father-and-son combo arrived and took their seats, followed by two other men he was pretty sure he'd seen the other day at Hank's, the tackle shop attached to the diner in Keystone Ridge, where he'd driven out last week to staple an advertisement for the class to the bulletin board.

Jack pretended to busy himself at the front of the classroom while the students chatted easily among themselves, comparing recent expeditions and favorite spots to fish. He glanced at his watch. They were only missing one person, but it was already two minutes past the hour, so he figured he'd get the class underway and the late student could catch up on arrival.

He cleared his throat. "All right, I think we'll get started," he said, clapping his hands together. He surveyed the room. The five students staring back at him looked exactly like the guys who patronized his fly-fishing expedition business: Seasoned pros visiting the Bow River to access what was widely considered one of the best fly-fishing locations in North America. Eager newbies wanting to learn a skill and get a trophy shot that would garner some likes on social media. Bachelor parties where the focus was more on the beer than on the fishing itself. Jack always appreciated the fraternity in those groups, especially when it meant he could quietly do his thing without the pressure to fill in the gaps in conversation.

"I'm Jack Wallace. I own Wallace Expeditions, and I've been fly-fishing since I could stand stabilized in the Athabasca," he said to a few chuckles. "Over the next three weeks, we're going to learn the basics of a few classic flies. Obviously you can buy all of these premade," he said, gesturing to an image from a local provider's website projected on the whiteboard, "but there's something really satisfying about making one on your own. And you can't beat the quality." He moved to pick up the vise from the instructor's desk and noticed a few of the students' attention had shifted to the entrance of the classroom.

"Sorry I'm late," Jack heard from behind him and turned toward the classroom entrance to find a woman who seemed to be doing her best to enter the room with as little fanfare as possible. She had dark, wavy shoulder-length hair, deep green eyes, and carried a giant handbag and an almost equally giant purple travel mug with a pink straw sticking out of it. She slid into the chair at the closest desk to the door, which was not one of the desks Jack had set up with class materials. Flashing him a quick, apologetic smile, she started to unload various items from her Mary Poppins bag.

He glanced down at his class list for the only remaining name. "C. McCarthy?" he asked.

"That's me," she said. "Celeste. Sorry—my sister dropped me off at the wrong building, so by the time I figured it out and called her to come back, I was already late. I'm all set, though," she said, motioning toward the entire suite of materials she'd set up on her desk—a tablet with a wireless keyboard, a notebook, a graphing calculator—none of which would be required for the evening's session.

Jack cleared his throat. "All right," he said, sensing the rest of his class's impatience and amusement. "Glad you could join us."

This was not the C. McCarthy he'd pictured when running through the list only moments ago. Maybe a Chris, a Cameron, a Carlos, or a Cooper. He tried to mask his surprise and reminded himself not to make assumptions. While most of his clientele were dudes, over the years he'd seen a big uptick in women signing up for his tours too. He was happy to see the sport diversify and hoped it continued to do so. Who wouldn't love being out on the river, surrounded by sparkling water and the possibility of a great catch?

Still, this seemed like a bit of a stretch. Celeste appeared to be in her late twenties or early thirties, and in a dark blue dress that cut off right above the knee and a pair of ankle boots that didn't look anywhere near weatherproof, she wasn't really dressed the part.

Jack ran his fingers through his hair, then returned to where he'd set himself up for instruction. He'd just started to relax, and now he felt his nerves getting all whipped up again under his new student's expectant gaze. "Come on and join us over here," he said, motioning toward the empty station. "I don't think you'll need any of that stuff."

He cleared his throat again to address the larger group. "So, I'll just start with a brief history of the craft, just to, uh, give us some context." As he spoke, Jack watched out of the corner of his eye as Celeste peered over at the small piles of hooks, different-colored feathers and string, her pretty features all scrunched up with confusion. "The earliest-recorded flies date back to 200 AD, but the major advancements in the tradition were from nineteenth-century England." He moved a slide forward to show the cover of

The Way of a Trout with a Fly, a classic guide from the 1920s. For a second Jack felt kind of teacherly and knowledgeable and would have likely been starting to relax if it weren't for the pair of big green eyes looking at him as though he were nuts.

"Excuse me—sorry," Celeste interrupted. She looked around at the group apologetically, then back at Jack. "But what does this have to do with accounting?"

He paused as the man with the beard chuckled. "Uh, this has nothing at all to do with accounting," Jack said. Five minutes into class and he already had a troublesome pupil. Why his family did this for a living was beyond him.

Celeste narrowed her eyes. "But that's the course I signed up for."

Now the calculator made sense. "Well, you're in the wrong place," Jack said.

With her lips pursed, she tapped her phone, then crossed the classroom and flashed the screen at him. "Here's my registration confirmation." Celeste was standing close enough that he could pick up on the notes of her perfume or shampoo or something really nice smelling. Whatever it was made him take a deep, steadying breath in.

Jack glanced quickly at her phone. "Not sure. Maybe you signed up for the wrong class. You're welcome to stick around. But I have nothing to do with scheduling, and the office is closed for the day, so…"

"But I need to learn about OTAs." Celeste's eyes, which

had been flashing with annoyance, now betrayed the slightest bit of desperation. Jack found himself wishing he knew anything about OTAs so he could do this beautiful woman a favor or at least move on with his class.

"I'm sorry. Not sure I can help you there," he said. He'd do pretty much anything else she asked, though.

Celeste sighed. "My sister registered me. She must have made a mistake. And my other sister dropped me off. She has my car, and she's at knitting club now, so I can't leave anyway." She looked up at him and then pursed her lips in a tight smile. "Sorry for the life story. I'll just sit."

Was this how all first days of class went? Best-laid plans, blown over by erroneously enrolled, incredibly attractive women? He waited for a moment as she returned her supplies to her backpack, then tentatively joined the rest of the group, who acknowledged her with polite nods and murmured greetings. Celeste flipped her hair over her shoulder and flashed him a quick smile.

His throat grew tight. "All right, then. Take two." Jack picked up a hook from the desk in front of him and held it up for the group. "Let's start with this: size-five Alex Jackson Steelhead Iron," he said. "You can use a Gamakatsu, Daiichi, or TMC, but I personally prefer this brand. Sizes go from two to six, but for our first attempt we'll stick to something on the larger size, since it's easier to handle."

"Why not go with the six, then?" Celeste said. "Since we're beginners?"

Jack stared at Celeste, while the son in the father/son combo shot her a look. "They were sold out."

Celeste raised an eyebrow, a light challenge mixed with a note of *I know I'm getting a rise out of you*, and Jack was torn between showing her the door and asking for her number. Beautiful, outspoken, and just a little bit needy—in another life, she was just the kind of woman he'd have pursued relentlessly. Judging from the spark that he felt after only minutes of interaction, he was sure it wouldn't have been a challenging proposition. But that was another life. In this one, there was no space for a heartbreaker like C. McCarthy.

Despite the electric charge in the air, Jack was somehow able to focus back on the task at hand and proceeded to show the group some basics about weaving the threads around the hook and how to securely attach a feather. After thirty minutes, each member of the class had figured out a basic fly. Even Celeste, who managed to make the tidiest one of the group. "My sister would love this," she said to Jack as he inspected her tie, which she held up between two glossy painted-pink fingernails. "She's obsessed with old-timey things."

"Old timey, huh?" he said. "I prefer the term *timeless*. It's endured because it works." Celeste didn't reply, and Jack watched as she intently fixed a blue feather to finish off her creation.

"You could catch a nice trout with that fly," he said. "Very tidy. Expert construction." He wasn't lying.

Celeste scrunched her nose. "I'm not really into fishing. Much to my father's disappointment."

"He's a fisherman?"

"He's an everything outdoorsman. The nature bug skipped me. My sister's a biology professor and researcher, though. And my other two sisters like being outside. So, he always had someone to drag out in the heat or rain or snow. I'm the disappointing indoorsy daughter."

Jack noted her makeup and her smooth, fair skin. It didn't surprise him that she didn't spend too much time outside.

"Well, it would be a shame for that to go to waste," he said, motioning toward her completed tie. "You should come on down to the river tomorrow and give it a go." He saw a glint in her eye before he looked over to the rest of the group. "That goes for everyone," he said. "I take groups out on the Bow near the bend at Castle Rock, Tuesdays through Saturdays. As my students, I'll give you the family-and-friends rate."

Nothing wrong with trying to drum up a little extra business through his class. God knows he needed it. Bookings for the spring were dismal, and in the last couple of years, competition in the area had increased exponentially. Teaching this class wasn't going to save his business, but it would help fill in a bit of a gap in revenue for the time being.

"Thanks for the invite. But I'll be working," Celeste said.

He hadn't expected her to take him up on the offer, so

he wasn't sure why he felt a pang of disappointment. "What's work for you?"

"I manage the Butterfly Lake Lodge, just outside of Keystone Ridge," she said.

"I've heard of it." The lodge had a reputation for being elegant and romantic. Not really the type of establishment his clients stayed when they came to town for his expeditions. But he could definitely picture Celeste fitting in at a place like that.

He gave the class a sneak peek of the fly they'd be making next week, then gave them some instructions for packing their kits, which they could take home with them and bring back next week.

It was gratifying to see the group progress under his instruction. And he'd be lying if he said that it hadn't been fun to have Celeste around.

He bid the class good night, then Celeste approached him at the front of the class. "Thanks for putting up with me," she said and held out her kit. "It wasn't exactly how I pictured spending my evening, but at least if I ever get stranded in the middle of nowhere, I'll know I can survive."

Jack picked up a spare hook from his pile of resources and pressed it into her palm, her soft warmth sending a thrill dancing along his skin. "You'll need this. Not too many of these in the wild. And keep that," he said, motioning to her kit. "Maybe your sister will want to give it a go."

She accepted the hook from his hand and grinned. "I'll

keep it in my pocket. And Quinn will love this. Good night, Jack."

He suddenly realized that if Celeste dropped out, there might not be a class next week. "Wait," he said. "Are you— Is there some way I could convince you to come back next week?" He could figure out a way to manage all the ways Celeste was undoing him if it meant he could keep his business afloat.

She turned around and looked at him quizzically. "Why?"

Jack's mind raced. "Next week we're making Jack Pines. It would make a great gift. For your dad. You can frame it." *Not bad.*

The sides of her mouth turned up slightly, ramping up the nerves in the pit of his stomach. "I need to take this accounting class. Or I'd think about it," she said. "Good night," she added and waved before leaving him standing alone in the empty classroom.

The evening had gone well. Really well. It was too bad his class might be canceled now that Celeste was dropping out.

Maybe he could convince one of the regulars down at Hank's to register. He'd go down there in the morning and drum up another student.

Before locking up the classroom, he looked out the window and saw Celeste getting into an SUV, her giant bag barely making it through the passenger-side entrance. He couldn't help but smile to himself, picturing her out on the river, her dress tucked into neoprene waders and a ball cap over her thick, glossy hair.

He shook his head. *Your students will always keep things interesting*, he heard his mom's voice in his head.

Celeste McCarthy? She was interesting, all right.

Just the kind of interesting he needed to avoid.

Chapter Three

"YOU'RE LATE," CELESTE said, sliding into the passenger seat of her Jeep Compass. Quinn sat at the steering wheel, a lollipop stick hanging out of her mouth and Ella Fitzgerald blaring from the speakers. Quinn's car was a vintage 1967 Mini Cooper in British Racing Green, which not only broke down every few months but could only safely operate on the roads from May to October when there was no snow on the ground, so in the in-between season she was always borrowing Celeste's or their parents' vehicles.

"It's 8:08," Quinn said.

"Class ended at eight." Celeste reached over and turned down the music.

"Does that mean I can't take your car next week?"

"Well," Celeste said, tucking the kit of materials into her tote bag, then pulling on her seat belt, "I won't be coming next week. Here, at least. Ava scheduled me for the wrong class."

"Oh no," said Quinn. "She's always in such a rush."

It was true. Despite Ava's brilliance, she had a tendency to quickness which sometimes made her overlook details—

everywhere except for in her spreadsheets.

"So what did you do, just sit there? You could have called me."

"It's all right. I knew you were busy." Quinn had met up with her knitting group at a café in Canmore. She often got a ride with one of the others in the group, but Elsa had just undergone a hip replacement and was still in the hospital. "I stayed in the class I showed up to. It was pretty random."

Someone exiting the building caught her eye. It was the cute instructor, carrying a milk crate with the materials from the class. "That was the teacher, actually," she said.

Quinn slowed the car to a stop and craned her neck. "Ohh, he's dreamy," she said. "He's giving me Cary Grant vibes, *His Girl Friday* era."

"Drive," Celeste said, laughing. "He's going to see us." She glanced back at Jack, watching as he balanced the milk crate while he fiddled with his keys, then put everything into the passenger side of his truck. He looked up as they drove by and gave Celeste a quick wave, the corners of his mouth turning up in a delicious grin. She waved back, the buzz of attraction that had struck her the moment she'd walked into the classroom showing no signs of fizzling out. Maybe it was a good thing he wasn't going to be her instructor. She'd have a hard time being a focused pupil.

Quinn navigated onto the main highway leading back to the lodge. Daylight savings time meant the clocks had moved forward an hour a few weekends before, so the unseasonably warm early-spring days were blessedly longer now, and the tree line glowed tangerine with the late setting sun. "What was so random about it?"

"Two words: fly-fishing."

"They teach fly-fishing at the college? That *is* random."

"No, not the actual fishing. It's a whole class on making these doodad fishing-tackle thingies. Here," she said, digging hers out of her pocket.

Quinn glanced away from the road, and her eyes widened when she saw Celeste's fly. "OMG! I love that! Those feathers are gorgeous."

"I knew you would. I told Jack." Celeste rolled her eyes.

"*Jack.*" Her sister made an exaggerated kissing sound. "Can I put it on my Insta when we get home?"

"Knock yourself out," Celeste said. Quinn ran a popular social media account called For Old Times' Sake, which partly focused on DIY in the old-timey—*timeless*—way of doing things, like making soap, using sourdough starters, and darning socks, and profiling her love of all things vintage and old, from movies and music to antiques and trinkets to old-school table etiquette. It blew Celeste's mind that Quinn had over one hundred thousand followers, but she was proud of her sister. If it weren't for the fact that she was glued to her phone most of the day, she might have been mistaken for someone who'd been plunked down in the twenty-first century by a time machine.

"But seriously, that guy was hot," Quinn said. "Debonair

meets outdoorsy. Like an L.L.Bean model or something."

Celeste had to agree with her sister, even though she didn't say it out loud. Jack was handsome, in a just-rolled-out-of-bed-but-owning-it rugged kind of way. And she liked the way his eyes looked like he was always smiling, even when he wasn't.

She stared out the window at the forested highway that would soon be blanketed in darkness. This wasn't a time to be daydreaming about hot teachers. She had a career to hang on to. And for the first time in her life, it was going to be up to her to make things happen.

QUINN PULLED CELESTE'S SUV into the parking area behind the lodge, where the McCarthys all kept their vehicles, next to the main house where Everett, Jeannie, and Quinn lived and the small cabin a little farther down the path that Jeannie and Everett had built for Celeste when she'd shared her intentions to work at the lodge. They'd wanted her to have some space of her own, and she'd agreed that it would be most convenient to be on the property for any emergencies or issues that arose.

When Everett had initially proposed he construct a cabin for her in her midtwenties, she hadn't been certain if it would be too close to her parents' place. But they gave her the space she needed, and it was handy to be close to work…and to her mother's pantry.

They walked the path together until the fork that divided the main house and Celeste's cabin. "'Night," Quinn said. "What's on for tomorrow?"

"Wedding prep," said Celeste. "And I have to get this course sorted out."

"'Kay, love you. If you need anything let me know."

"See you tomorrow," she said. "Actually, I could use your help with something."

"Shoot," said Quinn.

"Apparently the bride is some kind of social media influencer." Celeste had only found out because the groom had emailed her separately from the main email chain they had going on with wedding plans. He wanted to surprise his fiancée by releasing some butterflies at the end of the ceremony, which he thought she'd love and would be great content for her account.

Celeste had to break it to him that the local butterflies, which were omnipresent in the summer due to the unusual concentration of knapweed thistles, bee plants, and willow-herbs growing thick in a meadow near the south shore, were wrapping up their time in Mexico for the winter. She'd given him a few other ideas for visually interesting surprises, including a fresh-flower chandelier that could hang in the lodge's great room (something she'd seen on Pinterest and had always thought would look stunning) or a VW bus owned by the local brewery that could be ordered to various events and would serve pints and soft-pretzel poutine from the window.

"Who is she?" asked Quinn, opening her phone.

Celeste pulled her notebook from her purse and flipped through the pages. "Kassie Harris. Her handle is @KassieOnTheMove."

Quinn tapped on her phone, then her eyes widened in surprise. She looked up at Celeste. "Wowee. Let's make sure the lodge is showing at its best this weekend."

"What? Why?"

Quinn flashed her phone at Celeste. "Half mil followers. Looks pretty glam."

Celeste grabbed the phone from her sister's hands and scrolled through Kassie's social media profile. It was a mix of fitness, food, hair and makeup looks, outfits, and most recently, wedding planning, all curated with a consistent pale pink look to tie everything together. Many of the posts were sponsored content, and Celeste recognized the names of some musicians and professional athletes who followed the account.

Obviously the Butterfly Lake Lodge was about to be featured heavily on Kassie's account, and Celeste had to make sure that it not only showed at its best. This weekend, she would make it sparkle.

THE LODGE WAS quiet and still when she let herself in the mudroom door the next morning. Six rooms were occupied, and it seemed like everyone was still asleep.

It was at these quiet times of day that Celeste could take a moment to assess the lodge and its common spaces and make sure everything was just so.

In her mind, the Butterfly Lake Lodge was the most perfect vacation spot on the planet. The fact that Jeannie and Everett had kept the lodge as a small, family-run establishment was part of the appeal for their guests, many of whom were return visitors. They came from as far as New Zealand, Belgium, and Hong Kong, and no matter where they came from or who they were, they were welcomed with open arms. There was even a couple, the Hendersons, who for many years had stayed at the lodge every August twenty-second, despite the fact that they lived a four-minute walk down the street. The twenty-second was Sharon Henderson's birthday, and until last year, her late-husband Leigh had booked it as a gift for her because she loved nothing more than the warm cinnamon buns that would appear at her door in the morning that they would take back to bed and enjoy while lying in the soft Frette sheets with a hot coffee.

Celeste moved through the space quietly, tidying the tourism pamphlets and fluffing the pillows on the chairs.

The lodge had some modern touches but maintained a traditional, timeless feel with the restoration of classic details, such as the stained-glass window panels at the top of the picture windows and the oil lamps that lit the path from the parking lot to the reception area. There was also the old stone fireplace that was only dim during the warmest summer days and even then would often be lit for a few hours in the evening, when the mountain air shifted from humid to frigid on a dime.

She left the front reception and entered one of the lodge's most popular rooms, the puzzle room. It was a small nook off the great room, which housed a collection of jigsaws in a tall glass curio cabinet. The room also contained floor-to-ceiling shelves lined with the McCarthys' vast collection of paperback mysteries, a love shared by the whole family.

Just off the reception area and before the great room, in an alcove that opened to a covered porch, was the inn's pub, the Errant Elk. It was named after an incident the night of the last traditional Carmichael Christmas party in 1978, where an inebriated elk had wandered in through some open doors, surprising the guests and requiring quick thinking on Everett and Jeannie's part to lure it back outside. Now the pub was a cozy spot for the guests to order a pint and play darts or pool. It opened now and then to the public for an open mic night or intimate event.

Outside, there was a climate-battery greenhouse, where Everett puttered every morning, and their newest building, the gallery, a light-filled space near the water where local artists could showcase their work and where art workshops and book-club meetings were hosted.

And then there was the office, the least attractive and scenic room in the lodge but where Celeste spent the majority of her time. After making her morning to-do list, which she fastened to her clipboard, she picked up the phone and dialed the number for the college.

"We're very sorry for the error, Ms. McCarthy," said the woman who'd picked up the phone. "We'd be more than happy to move you to the Accounting for Beginners class, but the only option available at this point is an online course on Sundays at noon."

Celeste considered. Sunday afternoon was the busiest checkout time, and since the cleaning staff had Mondays off, there were always extra chores to delegate and pitch in to get the lodge in good shape for the week.

But then again, there would be no lodge or hotel work for her if she didn't get some sort of accreditation.

"Okay, that's fine," she said. She noted the details for the class on a sticky note, then hung up and went to the kitchen to get a snack. As she approached, she heard her parents speaking in hushed tones. She paused by the entrance.

"Personally, I think the sooner the better, so we can start making plans," she heard Jeannie say.

There was a moment of quiet. "Do you think we should just do one more Christmas? I think the girls would really appreciate it," Everett said.

"And sell in the winter? Forget it. The lodge will show perfectly in July."

More quiet. Celeste's mind raced. July? That was in less than three months.

"July's too soon to get everything in order," her dad said. "I think August could work. Probably September or October."

Celeste cleared her throat loudly, waited a beat, and then entered the kitchen. "Hey," she said.

Her parents were sitting at the kitchen island, a coffee in front of her dad and a tea steeping in front of her mom. It wasn't an unfamiliar scene, and if she didn't know better, she'd have just thought they were having their regular morning sit-down together.

"Good morning," her dad said in a forced chipper voice. He was wearing his old blue Patagonia fleece and a pair of khaki pants, his silver hair poking out from under a gray beanie.

Her mom stood up. "Can I get you something, honey?" In contrast, Jeannie wore her "uniform": black leggings with a long crisp white dress shirt over top and clogs with an apron, her gray hair in an angled bob. Celeste's parents got away with a more casual attire because of their responsibilities around the property, but Celeste, as the face of the lodge, generally wore a dress or a suit, something elegant and well-tailored. "A snack or a drink or something? I can make you an omelet."

What she really wanted was for her parents to stop acting so weird.

"Just getting myself a coffee," she said.

"Croissant with that?" her mom said. Everett pulled out a chair for her.

"Uh, sure," Celeste said and grabbed a mug to fill with black coffee. "I'll have it in the office, though. Where's everyone else?"

"Elodie's on a virtual panel until noon, Ava took Sam on a hike with some friends, and Quinn is over at the house."

So, she got the unenviable task of hanging out with her parents with a curtain of awkwardness in the air. She took a sip of her coffee and accepted the plate her mom passed her.

"Quinny told us about your class last night. Fly tying! Maybe I should join you," Everett said.

"It was kind of fun, actually," she said. "Too bad it's completely useless to me." She thought about the glint in Jack's eye when he'd complimented her work. "Turns out I was pretty good at it, though."

"No surprise there," Jeannie said. "You've always been good at whatever you put your mind to."

Celeste looked up at both of her parents beaming at her. It was time to go. "I'm going to go check over the table-and-chair rental and catering order for the wedding."

The soon-to-be-Instagram-famous family wedding for the upcoming weekend was a property buyout for the young couple and a group of twenty-four family members and close friends, exactly the number of rooms required to house the group, with both the ceremony and reception set to take place in the great room. She'd already checked it over twice an hour earlier, but she couldn't take another minute of her parents looking at her like she was as fragile as crepe paper.

Back in the quiet of the office, she picked up her phone, clicked on Instagram, and started some mindless scrolling. She smiled and shook her head when she saw that Quinn had already posted a photo of her fly and a short description of the craft followed by a number of hashtags like *#DIY* and *#HandCrafted*.

She also saw that Quinn had tagged a company called Wallace Expeditions in the photo. Celeste clicked on the tag, which brought her to the page of a local fly-fishing outfitter and tour guide. The very first photo was of Jack, standing in a knee-deep river and holding up a fishing rod and some kind of big fish, grinning widely, the forest emerald green behind him. The description below the photo advertised the upcoming season's expeditions.

Celeste zoomed in on the photo, on Jack's bright eyes and confident grin, and felt a warm tingle of desire dance through her core. The picture had likely been taken in the summer; his skin was nicely tanned, and he wore a T-shirt with his company logo, his sleeves clinging to his sturdy, muscular upper body.

She thought back to that brief moment when she thought he'd invited her to join him on the river. Just her, not the entire class. Not that wading through freezing-cold water in the late-April drizzle to try to catch a fish that could be easily purchased at the local grocery store or fishmonger had any iota of appeal to it, but she'd felt silly that she'd thought for a split second that the invite had been specific to her—the woman who'd worn a dress to Fly-Tying 101.

Jack was for sure the kind of guy who favored women who liked backpacking and sleeping outside and wearing the same clothes for days on end. Celeste and that whole scene were two opposing poles of a magnet.

Not that dating was a priority right now. The coming months needed to be focused on setting herself up for continued employment and helping her sisters through what would be a challenging time for their family. And then there were her parents. They were clearly trying to appear to be fine for their sake, but surely they'd both be dealing with many complex emotions over the course of the sale. All Celeste could hope was that things proceeded as smoothly as possible.

There was no time to dabble in fantasies of nature-loving men who hooked fish for a living.

Was there anything wrong with a little daydreaming, though? She navigated back to Quinn's post and hit *Like*, then threw her phone onto the table and looked around the office, trying to decide what to do next.

"I knew you liked him," a voice sounded from directly over her shoulder, causing her to yelp and drop her phone. She whirled around to find Quinn, a satisfied grin on her face. "And I don't blame you."

"I was just looking at your post. For god's sake," Celeste said, pinching her sister on her forearm.

"I bet you're counting down until Monday."

"Actually, I just called the college to ask them to transfer my class."

"Too bad," Quinn said. "He's like the first guy who's made you blush since Matt."

Celeste shot her sister a look. "I don't want to talk about Matt," she said. "And he didn't make me blush."

"Uh-huh," Quinn said.

"When did you become such a brat? That's Ava's job." She sat back in her chair. "Don't you have some mothballs to tend to? A penny farthing to ride into town? Candlesticks to drip?"

Quinn took a strip of licorice from Celeste's desk and went to exit the room, then turned around. Her expression changed from playful to serious. "You know, not all guys are dicks like Matt. You really should start dating again sometime soon. Even if it's not Professor Dreamy."

"Thanks for the life talk, small fry. Maybe you'll take your own advice soon and join the twenty-first century."

"I'm only twenty-seven. People my age don't date."

"I don't want to know what that means," said Celeste. "Close the door on your way out."

Quinn took an exaggerated bite of her licorice and grinned before closing the door. Celeste spent a few minutes sending emails and surveying the reservations for the next few weeks. After the wedding that weekend, they were about 75 percent booked for the next month, which was quite good for the early spring. Once the summer came around, they'd be operating at capacity, with a healthy waiting list, for May through August and often a couple of weeks into September. Their prices reflected the busy season but were never unreasonable, and the online ratings, Quinn's social media–marketing efforts, and the praiseworthy press they'd received in publications like *Travel and Leisure*, the *Globe Travel*, and even a mention in the *Goop* travel section always ensured the Butterfly Lake Lodge was on people's radar.

Celeste knew she was a key part of the lodge's success. There was no guarantee, however, that the new owner would want to keep the lodge the same. She needed to solidify her plan B.

She opened up a local job-search board, but most of the postings were for server or housekeeping positions. Instead, she went on individual hotel and resort websites to see what might be posted, but again, no luck.

After doing a quick walk around of the lodge to check in on guests and staff, she popped in her earbuds, pulled on a light jacket and set off down the gravel road to get a few steps in, and make a phone call she didn't want eavesdropped on.

The sun was high in the sky, but the forecast was calling for rain that afternoon. Every conversation in the area lately started with remarks about how early spring had come this year. Usually there would be snow on the ground and frozen lakes until mid-May, but this year, the snow had already disappeared and people were cautiously optimistic that they'd made it through the winter.

Regardless, it was always four seasons in one day in the mountains, so there was a chance on her short walk she'd either be shedding her jacket if it got too warm or popping open her umbrella to shield herself from rain or hail.

When she was a safe enough distance from the lodge, she selected Gus Evans's phone number from her address book. Gus was the lead concierge at the Halcyon Retreat Center two lakes over...and the area's biggest gossip. If anyone had the scoop, it would be him.

"Why, are you looking?" Gus whispered as soon as Celeste inquired about any openings he might be aware of.

"Uh, no, why would I be looking?" she said, hoping she sounded convincing. "I'm just...curious."

"Hold on—let me move to the back office," Gus said, and Celeste heard shuffling in the background, then a door closing. "Okay. You didn't hear it from me, but word has it that Annie Flint is retiring at the end of the next month."

"You're kidding."

"Not kidding. My sources tell me she's moving to Palm Beach. She's had a boy toy there all these years, and she's finally agreed to retire and move in with him."

Celeste's mind whirled. Annie Flint was renowned in the area as the iron lady at the front desk of the Keystone Ridge

Resort, the area's most storied and expensive luxury hotel. There were rumors she used a UV light to inspect the cleanliness of her employees' uniforms before every shift, and most people took it as a general fact that Annie would be queen of the castle until the day they rolled her dead body out the inn's service door.

"Okay, that's some hot gossip," Celeste said. "Anyway, see you at the BIA meeting next month?"

"Maybe. We're short-staffed here, so I've been working doubles twice a week. I might have to miss the boxed wine and stale shortbreads this time around. Gotta go."

Celeste hung up and took a deep breath of the fresh early-spring air. Right on cue, a gentle mist started to fall. She pulled on her hood and opened her umbrella and decided to keep walking a little longer to burn off some nervous energy.

The Keystone Ridge Resort could be an interesting opportunity. It belonged to a large chain and they had their own business office, so the role was probably more about bookings and some concierge work, which she was sure she could talk through without official credentials.

She did an internet search of the resort on her phone, then zoomed in on the write-up of the amenities and offerings and types of packages they offered. Honeymooners, family getaways, weddings…she knew all about those. She scrolled down farther to find that the Keystone also hosted some of the most exclusive hunting-and-fishing expeditions in the area. Annie Flint could probably tie a Silver Blue in her sleep.

Would it be helpful to stay in Jack's class, to learn a bit more about the sport, to be able to casually drop some lingo in an interview and converse with her clientele? It wouldn't hurt—that was for sure.

With the lodge at 75 percent over the coming weeks, she could definitely handle the online accounting course and Jack's class. Besides, tying flies was kind of fun.

She would do it. A night away from the lodge and her strangely behaving parents, and a new way to connect with her guests, wherever she ended up working. And if the rumors were true about Annie Flint's retirement, she'd have to start getting her resume together too.

The mist turned to rain. Celeste turned back toward the lodge and picked up her pace.

Things were falling neatly into place—just as she liked it.

Chapter Four

JACK SPOONED FRESHLY ground coffee beans into his French press and filled it up with boiling water from the kettle, then gazed out the window at the steady rain beating down on the thick pine forest outside of his house while he waited for the grounds to steep.

His house was a well-built riverside bungalow he'd bought three years earlier from a family of four moving to Ottawa. It sat one hundred feet from the upper Bow River, which flowed from Bow Lake and Banff, snaking down through the Rockies all the way south of Calgary. He had neighbors on both sides, with enough forest in between for everyone to have their privacy but still feel like there were people to rely on if someone needed a cup of sugar or help picking up mail while they were on vacation. This stretch of the river was sandwiched between Sandpiper Springs, a small, gritty lumber town, to the north and Keystone Ridge to the south.

The house had three bedrooms, one of which he used to sleep, another which served as his office, and the third where he kept his bookshelves and a big comfy couch as well as a

Murphy bed for when his brother, Caden, came to visit from Surrey with his wife, Julie, and their one-year-old girl, Millie.

There'd been a point when those rooms had been meant to serve a very different purpose. But after Christine had broken things off and left town, he couldn't bring himself to sell. He liked the quiet of the forest, the way the light trickled through the trees, and the burble of the river at night when he left the windows open a crack.

Every now and then a memory of sitting out on the porch drinking coffee with Christine flashed in his mind, but it had been two years since she'd left and he'd gotten used to having his coffee solo.

It was the perfect home as far as Jack was concerned, but the rising interest rates on his variable-rate mortgage and the steady increase in property taxes that kept up with the area's increasing popularity meant that if business didn't pick up soon, he might have to downsize to something smaller in town.

He poured himself a cup of coffee in a travel mug, then whistled for Bodie, his ten-year-old Siberian husky, who leapt from his bed in front of the wood-burning fireplace, panting in anticipation of his morning walk. Only a dog would be that excited to leave a cozy spot in front of the fire to go out in the damp early-spring rain, and lucky for Bodie, inclement weather never phased Jack. He was as happy outside in the snow or sleet as he was on a radiant sunny day. He lived to be outside—another reason why his parents hadn't been able to convince him to pursue teaching or some other kind of corporate job.

The days he wasn't working played out the same way: morning walk with Bodie, followed by a trip into town for errands. Then he'd get some chores done at home and do some cooking and listen to a podcast or watch something on Netflix.

His life was quiet and predictable, but it suited him. And he got enough people time from his job anyway—at least when he had customers.

Before leashing up Bodie, Jack opened his laptop and took a sip of his coffee while the machine booted up. He crossed his fingers that the couple hundred bucks he'd dumped into social media advertising, at his brother's urging, had resulted in a few bookings.

No luck.

Now he was out the cost of two registrations. He grunted in frustration and pushed the laptop closed. "Come on, Bodie," he said.

It was misty and gray out, but the frigid temperatures had recently been making way for a warmer but damper early spring.

Jack always kept his dog on a leash when they walked. Bodie would love to run free through the woods, chasing squirrels and field mice, but there was always a chance they'd encounter a bear or a cougar, and Jack's home was empty enough without him losing Bodie too.

When they reached the river, Jack stopped in his tracks. "What in the goddamn hell," he grunted and gripped Bodie's leash tightly. The husky must have felt the current of anger right through the leash to his collar, and he started barking at the figure out on the river.

Standing in fresh-out-of-the-box waders and holding a fishing rod was Forrest Halpern, one of the most privileged twentysomethings in the area, who'd recently gotten a huge influx of cash from his daddy to fund the startup of his own wilderness-adventure company. Despite Forrest's lack of experience as an angler, his company was siphoning clients from Jack as quickly as a frosh with a beer funnel at a frat party.

Jack had heard that he was fully booked all summer, thanks to a series of TikTok and Instagram videos he'd hired a production company to make. Forrest had the experience of Jack's baby toe, and he couldn't believe the charlatan was capitalizing on zero training.

And now he was parading right in front of Jack's place. It was for sure on purpose. Forrest had hated him since Jack had made a side comment to Forrest's father at a town meeting about his son's rumored side hustle. Jack didn't have any evidence, but word from the guys at the tackle shop was that Forrest was moving cocaine, fentanyl, and methamphetamine around in Sandpiper Springs and the surrounding communities that were also on the rougher side, and he'd figured his dad would want to know.

Kendall Halpern, Forrest's dad and the owner of the province's largest logging company, had waved Jack off, but after a local high school kid had OD'd at a bush party and the police had questioned Forrest, Kendall had gotten involved and all charges had been dropped.

Now not only was Jack trying to make up ground for his slumping business, but he was competing with a sniveling douchebag who had infinite resources and was probably snorting any profits in powder form.

"Hey there, Wallace," Forrest called, giving him an exaggerated wave. "Hope you don't mind—I'm scouting out some new spots! You're not using this area these days, are you, bro?"

It's only my goddamn backyard, Jack wanted to say. *Bro.* "No. Not much action here, though," he said. Which Forrest would know if he knew anything about anything.

"I've got some Helios I'm looking to sell, if you need anything. Just picked up these new Sage X rods. Sweet, eh?"

Jack's blood boiled. He did need new equipment, but he'd never give Forrest Halpern the satisfaction of taking his castoffs. He gave Forrest a quick wave and kept walking, but not before noting the rookie cast he made, which was even more embarrassing given the quality of his rod, to the tune of at least two grand. Jack waited until he was far enough away to smirk to himself.

Forrest Halpern was the definition of a hack. Then again, clearly he was doing something right if people were employing his services. But this was the problem with the internet. It was too easy to buy five-star ratings on Google, to get eyes on your product, even when you were selling a load of crap. As long as Forrest could give travelers that Instagram shot, the quality didn't seem to matter.

Bodie stopped to sniff at what first looked like a pine cone but at closer inspection was the droppings of some kind of animal. "Come on, Bodie," Jack said. "We don't put shit up our noses."

Jack trudged down the path, mind whirling with how to pull his business out of the tank. He was skilled, he was knowledgeable, he knew how to read river conditions and wind patterns and just about any color sky and make a best guess about where to take his groups. Could Forrest do that? Was he really booking as many clients as he was letting on?

There was only one place to find out—where the gossip flew around faster than any hair salon or high school cafeteria.

Jack brought Bodie back to the house, got into his pickup truck, and drove into Keystone Ridge to Hank's Tackle Shop, where all the local anglers sat out front drinking coffee and trading shit talk. It was time to figure out what the hell was going on.

"THERE HE IS," a booming voice called from a yellow

Muskoka chair outside of Hank's. Jack had barely excited the truck but was happy to see Hank Dougherty, tackle shop owner and social convenor of a ragtag group of locals, four of whom were seated in the other Muskoka chairs that formed a circle outside of the shop. "Where ya been? That box of tippet you ordered came in over a week ago."

Jack didn't want to tell Hank that he hadn't been by because his booking calendar was emptier than a dry well. "Caught a bug there for a bit," he said. "Plus I've been teaching a class down at the college."

"I heard that," Hank said. "Good for you, Wallace."

"If you don't mind spreading the word, I've got a couple of spaces left in the class."

"Will do," said Hank.

"Hey, how's business been for you guys? Spring season picking up?"

"It's been steady," Hank said. "Lot of these newer companies dropping by, asking for discounts like they've been buying from me for years now. Like you. I told them they can ask again after they show me some loyalty." He took a sip from his coffee. "All I can say is that when I get a call for recommendations, yours is the first name I give 'em. But I don't know. Everyone's looking for a bargain these days, and some of these other guys are practically giving away their services. Not sure how much of a profit they're pulling in."

Jack considered. "Well, I appreciate that, Hank." The truth was some of them, like Forrest, were probably pulling in profits in different ways, but he wasn't going to be seen spreading rumors in a group like this. "Can I settle up?"

He followed Hank inside to the small tackle shop. The walls were lined with rods and reels, spools of line, apparel and every manner of hooks, weights, and tackle. Behind the counter was a wall full of photos of Hank and his staff members and customers holding trophy catches. The shop connected directly to Ronnie's Diner, which was owned and operated by Hank's wife, Veronica.

While Hank clicked on his computer, Jack glanced over to the diner's busy space, which, as always, was full of a mix of locals and tourists.

The enticing aroma of coffee grinds and bacon no doubt lured many visitors from the tackle shop, and despite the fact that he'd already had two coffees, Jack was considering plopping down at a table for Veronica's famous spinach-and-Monterey omelet.

He scanned the room for an empty table and stopped when his gaze settled right in the middle of the room, at a table with three women. Apparently someone had just said something very amusing because one of them was laughing so hard her head was buried in her hands, her shoulders convulsing in laughter.

When she looked up, Jack took a sharp breath in. It was Celeste McCarthy, with a wide grin on her face and tears of laughter in her eyes.

"That'll be two-eighty-two forty-nine," said Hank, sliding an invoice toward him. "I knocked 15 percent off."

"You didn't need to do that," Jack said as he slid his credit card across the counter. The last thing he wanted was people's charity. But still, he appreciated it. "Hey, uh, I'm just going to grab a quick bite. I'll pick everything up in a few minutes."

"I'll leave it by the door for ya. Thanks, Jack."

Jack tucked the receipt into his pocket and passed through the narrow doorway between the tackle shop and the diner. Celeste and the other two women appeared to be discussing something serious now. He almost turned around, not wanting to disrupt their conversation, but Celeste looked over and stopped midsentence, then sat up and smiled at him.

"Hey, Jack," she said.

He approached the edge of their table and nodded at Celeste and the two other women who, he could tell now that he was closer up, must've been her sisters. "My star student," he said. "Sorry you won't be joining us again."

"Actually," Celeste said, tilting her head to the side slightly and flashing him another grin, "I changed my mind. I'll see you on Monday."

Jack tried to mask his surprise, but knowing Celeste was sticking around in his class was...unexpected. "Well, I'm glad to hear that," he said. He looked at the two other women. "Jack Wallace."

"Sorry—that was rude of me," Celeste said. "These are

my sisters, Elodie and Quinn."

"Nice to meet you," Jack said.

They both had Celeste's bright eyes, but Elodie's hair was lighter and Quinn looked like she'd just stepped out of the 1960s, with a fringed leather vest and some kind of hippy-looking flower headband.

"I'm the one who tagged you on Instagram the other day," Quinn said. "The post is getting so many likes."

"Is that right?" Jack said. He liked the sound of that. Free publicity. "Well, you're welcome to come by the class too, if you'd like." Nothing wrong with getting a little more exposure on social media. Quinn appeared to be in her twenties and probably knew a whole hell of a lot more about it than he did.

Out of the corner of his eye, he could see Celeste shoot Quinn a look. "Really?" Quinn said. "I'd love to take some photos. As a follow-up post. Maybe with, like, a step-by-step of whatever you're making?"

"Absolutely," Jack said, flipping his keys in his hand. He noticed Celeste shift in her seat. "All right, well…"

"You're welcome to join us," said Quinn.

"Appreciate that. I'm just going to grab some takeout. Enjoy your meal, ladies," he said. He looked at Celeste. "See you in class."

"See you then," she said.

It was still gray and rainy outside as Jack made his way back to his truck, but suddenly the day felt a lot lighter.

AS SOON AS Jack was out of earshot, the teasing began. "Someone has a crush," said Elodie.

"Come on, can you blame her?" Quinn said. "That man is *Hollywood* hot." She fanned herself with her hand and pretended to swoon.

"Shut up, both of you," said Celeste. "What are you, middle schoolers?"

"If I were into men, I'd have to agree with Quinn," said Elodie, grinning.

Celeste shot her a look. Normally Elodie could be counted on to act mature, but Quinn was a bad influence.

"We need to figure out what you're wearing to class on Monday," said Quinn.

"I can dress myself, thank you very much. And you're not coming," Celeste said.

"Of course I'm coming! This is valuable content for my socials."

Celeste rolled her eyes and sat back in her seat. She loved her sisters, but they were pests.

"He's so into you," Quinn whispered excitedly. "He was practically undressing you with his eyes."

"Shut up," she said again.

Oscar, their usual waiter, a sixtysomething-year-old man with a tidy handlebar mustache, approached their table, notepad in hand. They'd been going to Ronnie's since they were kids, and Oscar had been there just about as long. "Ready to order, ladies?"

"Two eggs, over easy, hash browns, bacon, whole-wheat toast, and a black coffee," said Celeste, not bothering to look at the menu. "Maybe I should get decaf. I've already had two coffees this morning."

"Oh, no. Don't do that. Haven't you heard decaf has methylene chloride in it? That's a carcinogen," said Elodie, a horrified look on her face.

"You're such a hypochondriac," Celeste said. Elodie was always on the lookout for things that could kill her. "Fine, I'll have the caffeine."

"I'll have the mango benny, double espresso, and a waffle on the side," said Quinn. "And a cup of ice water to pour over my sister's head. She's all steamed up."

"Quinn," Celeste hissed.

Oscar paused, then looked at Elodie. "And let me guess—huevos migas, sub chips for the tortilla," he said. "And an Earl Grey tea."

"We love you, Oscar," said Elodie as Oscar left to put in their order. Hopefully it would be quick. After a late-night call to fix a running toilet, Celeste hadn't been able to get back to sleep and was now starving. With the lodge fully booked and both their parents flitting around the property, they'd decided to get off-site so they could dissect the situation without Jeannie and Everett overhearing them.

"I hate the idea that they've been unhappy just because

they worry about upsetting us."

"I'd have been okay with them holding on a little long-er," Celeste said. She was trying to focus on the conversation, but all she could think about was the interaction with Jack. His perfectly fit blue jeans and his heavy work coat and his tousled hair poking out from the edges of his wool toque, which only added to his rugged charm. That glint in his eyes, like a sudden spark waiting to ignite, that switched on a part of her that had been ignored for far too long.

When he'd emerged from the tackle shop, caught her eye, and waved, her stomach had just about bottomed out.

There was no denying she was attracted to him. But his type was all too common in the area, and even though the desire was undeniable, they were in no way compatible.

Celeste took after her mother in her level of interest in the outdoor-granola lifestyle, a level hovering at zero. Was it so wrong that she preferred a climate-controlled room and her down comforter over sleeping on rocky, uneven ground, with the threat of a bear attack always in the back of her mind? That she liked eating well-cooked food from sanitized dishes at a level table rather than gross camp food from a tin plate balanced on her lap?

Jack was exactly the kind of guy who looked down on people like Celeste. And even if he wasn't, she had one job right now, and that job required all her spare time and headspace.

"Earth to Celeste," Quinn said, waving a piece of waffle

on a fork in her face.

"Fine, you can come to the class with me," she said. "But if you do anything to embarrass me, you're never borrowing my car again."

"I'll behave. Scout's honor," Quinn said. She grinned. "But I was asking you to pass the ketchup."

Celeste's cheeks burned as her sisters erupted in laughter. "All right, laugh it up," she said and tossed a sugar packet across the table at Quinn. "You can pay for your own breakfasts."

Chapter Five

ON MONDAY EVENING, Celeste strode down the hallway at Oakview College balancing a container of freshly baked chocolate chip cookies she'd nicked from the rack Jeannie had made for happy hour, Quinn trailing behind her with her Pentax hanging from a strap around her neck.

Celeste paused outside of the classroom, finger combed her hair, then looked back at her sister before entering. "Make sure you get a good shot of me working," she said. If Quinn insisted on tagging along, she might as well be useful. Nothing wrong with getting a shot of her up on the Butterfly Lake Lodge social media pages, in case a prospective employer happened to look her up. She already had some hashtags in mind: *#LifelongLearning*, *#KnowledgeableHost*.

#HireMePlease, she thought.

"On it," said Quinn. "And you're looking extra cute today. Did someone spend time getting ready for class?"

"Quinn," Celeste warned. Maybe she'd taken a few minutes to add some waves to her hair with her curling iron and picked the white bodysuit she knew hugged her waist nicely with jeans. So what? She didn't get out much, so what was wrong with making an effort when she did? "Let's go."

All five other class members had already arrived and were seated with their materials laid out in front of them. Jack was perched on a desk, wearing a black sweater and army-green khakis, a pen tucked behind his ear and a smile on his face. As his gaze roamed over her, she couldn't help but revel in the sensation of his eyes tracing the contours of her outfit. He might've been into women who wore fleece and Gore-Tex, but he was only a man.

"She's back," said the man with the gray ponytail. Bryant, she remembered. "And she brought a friend!"

"Couldn't miss Jackpine week," Celeste said. "This is my sister, Quinn. She's here to take some photos."

"Great to see you back," Bryant said. "Glad you changed your mind."

The man beside him—George, was it?—held out his fist to bump against hers. Of all the places she'd never thought she'd find herself.

"I thought it wouldn't be a bad idea to acquaint myself with something that brings in a lot of tourism to the area." With Jack's gaze lingering on her, Celeste felt a tinge of nervousness tingling down her spine yet a newfound confidence rising within her. She stood up a bit straighter. "I know a lot of the local hotels cater to fishing trips. And it's always nice to be able to make conversation with guests about their interests."

"So does this mean that we're going to get you out on the river?" Jack said. His lips were turned up in a teasing smile. "Experiential learning at its best."

"Don't push it," Celeste said, even though the idea held the slightest bit more appeal if it involved spending more time with Jack.

"All right, well. Glad to have you back."

Quinn gave him a wave and approached the desks, which once again were set up with a variety of different feathers and string.

"Cool," Quinn said and immediately started snapping pictures.

Jack started the lesson and took them through another fly, a miniature blue feature tied with a yellow string on a black hook and a small piece of red fabric.

"We're actually going to make a Skirrow's Fancy today," Jack said, holding up his exemplar for the group to see. "We use seal's fur for this one. Gives it a nice buggy look but doesn't weigh it down."

"Seal's fur? How on earth did people figure out that this would attract fish?" Celeste asked.

"Trial and error, likely," said Jack. "Years and years of fishers making educated guesses. And it seems an unlucky trout took the bait on this one."

"It's a good lesson: Beware of things that attract you. They could also kill you."

Jack cocked his eyebrow. "Agreed."

What was that supposed to mean? She watched as he separated the strings in the pile in front of him. When he finally looked up, their eyes locked in a silent exchange that sent a shiver across the surface of her skin. She swallowed nervously.

Was Jack trying to tell her something? Had he been burned before?

She did her best to put the thought out of her head and focus on following along with the directions he was delivering. He was authoritative but not arrogant, and she liked how he stopped now and then to check in on everyone individually.

Halfway through the class, when one of the other students required help getting back on track, Celeste opened the container of cookies and pulled some napkins from her bag and circulated around the room.

"These are unbelievable," said George, after finishing his in two large bites. She held out the container again, inviting him to take another from the container.

Jack's face lit up with amusement. "You brought snacks?"

She used a napkin to pluck one from the container and passed it to him. "Nothing wrong with elevating the experience," she said. His hand brushed hers as he accepted the napkin, and even the slightest of contact was enough to send a tingle of desire dancing across the surface of her skin.

She watched as Jack took a bite, his expression changing to one of blissed-out satisfaction. "Ugh. Where'd you learn to bake like this?"

"I can't take credit other than for bringing them here. My mother made these," Celeste said. "Special order. They're a favorite of the guests at our lodge."

"I don't doubt it," he said.

"Wait until you try the cinnamon buns. They're the marquee dessert."

"I'd like to invite you to return next week."

Celeste couldn't help the smile from spreading across her lips. "For the desserts or the pleasure of my company?" she said.

"Both," said Jack, without missing a beat. Celeste was thankful Quinn was absorbed with something on the other side of the classroom and hadn't heard the exchange. She'd have a field day on the car ride home with this flirtation.

For the rest of the class, Celeste found herself enjoying herself more than she'd expected, and not just because it was fun being around Jack. It was nice to be away from the lodge and learning something new, despite not having much in common with the rest of her classmates.

Celeste had her head down and was focused on getting the final string tied as tightly as possible and felt a subtle shift in the air before realizing Jack was looking over her shoulder. She smoothed her hair, self-conscious with him so close and unable to shake off the flutter in her chest ignited by the weight of his gaze.

"You two get together," Quinn said, holding up her

camera. Of course she was right there to capture the moment.

Celeste shot her a look. "Actually, I think unposed photos are probably better."

"Best to have options," her sister said, smiling wide.

Celeste made a mental note to kill her later on, then looked sideways at Jack.

"Ready for your close-up?" he said. He ran his fingers through his hair and straightened his collar. "How many followers did you say you have again?"

"One hundred fifty K and climbing," Quinn said. "And my followers will love this." She winked at Celeste, who stood awkwardly next to Jack and smiled as she snapped away.

"Hold up the fly," Quinn instructed. "Now why don't you go back to your desk and pretend to be working again. Jack, you stand over her shoulder and pretend to give her an instruction."

"The things we do for our businesses," Celeste said, trying to sound humorous even though her nerves were dancing beneath the surface. Did Jack find this as awkward as she did? He seemed pretty comfortable. Maybe it was the having Jack so close to her, his alluring aftershave filling in the air around them that was making her so jittery.

"Closer," Quinn directed, and Celeste felt Jack's firm torso pressed up against her back. With a steadying breath, she forced herself to maintain composure, willing herself to appear unaffected by his proximity.

Her sister continued to take photos, giving directions here and there. "Okay, I think I've got what I need," she said. "I'll aim to get the post up by tomorrow night, and I'll tag your company and the college."

"Thank you," Jack said. "Appreciate it." He looked at Celeste. "And thanks for modeling."

By the end of the class, she had another perfectly executed fly, which Jack held up for the class to see. "I think you're ready for the intermediate class," he said.

"Oh," said Celeste. "I didn't realize there were multiple levels. Maybe I just have a really good instructor."

Despite Jack not being at all her type, it was a fun back-and-forth. When was the last time she'd engaged in some harmless flirtation anyway?

With Matt, they'd started out as classmates at university, and their relationship had evolved in what Celeste now knew had been a matter of convenience. They'd had similar friends, lived in the same area, liked doing the same things on weekends. Had there ever been a strong sense of attraction, playfulness, or magnetism? She didn't think so. It had burned when he'd broken things off, but in retrospect, staying together would definitely have been settling.

Once she had things in order in her life, maybe it would be time to start dating again. Her friend Lindsey had just employed a matchmaking service that she swore by. She could date someone in the city—it was only an hour's drive away—and it might be nice to have an excuse to drive in and go shopping and visit great restaurants.

For now, even though dating was nowhere near a priority, there was nothing wrong with some fun flirting with an attractive distraction.

MAYBE HIS PARENTS hadn't been so off base after all. Teaching wasn't half bad. Jack might even go as far as to describe it as fun.

All six of his students had been successful with the day's fly, and five of them were chatting among themselves about recent catches and plans for the spring season. When he glanced over at Celeste, she was listening politely and applying hand cream.

Jack could tell she spent a good amount of time on her appearance. Not in a way that made her look overly made up or vain, but there was a sheen to her that he imagined took some time to achieve. He liked it.

He'd thought it might be distracting and annoying to have a photographer in the class, but Quinn was professional and stayed out of everyone's way, and Jack was feeling optimistic about having his company featured on her profile.

Having Celeste back was no doubt a major contributing factor in how much he'd enjoyed the evening. More than once she'd caught him looking at her, even once dipping her chin and looking up at him with a knowing glance. It was adorable. It was flirtatious. It was irresistible.

And then there was the fact that she'd brought cookies for the group. The combination of her presence along with the gooey sweet dessert was making him forget all about the promise he'd made to himself. Was that all it took? Was he that weak?

Maybe he needed to do something about all this pent-up energy. Two years was too long to be alone.

He'd dated a few women after Christine had left but no one who had captured his attention. It was hard in this area anyway, where people knew each other and you ran the risk of running into an ex at the grocery store or the gym. In Jack's opinion, it wasn't worth the trouble.

He looked up at the clock and was surprised to see that it was already after eight p.m. The time had flown by, and it seemed like everyone else was so absorbed in their work and conversations they hadn't noticed either. "All right folks," Jack said. "Looks like time's up for tonight. You all did great work."

"We only have one class left. When do progress reports come out?" Celeste said.

"This isn't that kind of course. One hundred percent of your grade rests on the final exam."

"I'd better get studying," she said.

Out of the corner of his eye, Jack noticed Quinn laughing to herself. He didn't care. Being around Celeste was fun.

"See you next week, teach," said Celeste.

"See you next week," he echoed.

He was already counting down the days.

Chapter Six

O N THE MORNING that the Harris/Grant wedding party was due to check in, two days prior to the wedding, Celeste dragged herself out of bed shortly after five a.m.

She could have slept for another three or four hours, easily, but something she'd learned over time was that carving out an hour to herself before a weekend like the one that lay ahead was essential.

It was going to be a full-on four days, starting with welcoming guests and orienting them to the local area, assisting with last-minute wedding preparations, and finalizing the details for all the events leading up to Kassie and Jeff's dream wedding. Between now and Sunday afternoon, once everyone checked out after brunch, Celeste's life was going to be 100 percent consumed by the wedding, so she had to relish the few moments to herself before the workday began. Plus immediately after checkout on Sunday, she had her first accounting class.

She took her time under the spray of hot water in the shower, then got dressed for the day and crossed the parking area to the kitchen entrance for a coffee to take to the quiet of the great room.

When she entered the kitchen, she found Jeannie, apron covered with powdered sugar and phone cradled between her shoulder and ear. Her brow furrowed in what Celeste recognized as annoyance, something she didn't see often from her mother. "I thought he was supposed to be back this week," Jeannie said. "He was going to be the backup."

Uh-oh. The guests hadn't even arrived, and clearly they were already facing a hiccup.

"All right, well, send me his number, I guess," she said. "Goodbye."

Jeannie tossed her phone onto the counter beside a rack of cooling lemon tarts, then washed her hands in the sink. "Your father has a temperature of 101. He's in bed shivering. There's no way he'll be able to take the guys out tomorrow. I called Bill, but Aline said he stayed an extra week in Florida to golf. She gave me the name of some guy Bill hunts with. Jameson something?"

"Jameson Kent?" Celeste said, eyes widening. She'd met the local guide once at a town fundraiser at the local library, and he not only had the biggest, and most unfounded, ego she'd ever encountered, but she'd watched as he'd pocketed six sets of silverware in his parka pocket from one of the tables, for god knows what reason. There was no way they were allowing the groom and his family and friends to spend the day with that loser. "That's a hard no. I'd sooner take them out myself."

The day out was meant to happen while the bride, her mother and sisters, and the other female guests spent the day at the local hot-springs spa, then returned to the lodge for a specially designed happy hour, complete with a visit from a mixologist who was going to demo some signature cocktails, then stick around for the evening to mix drinks for the rehearsal dinner.

The rehearsal dinner was an elaborate seafood feast, a McCarthy-family specialty modeled after the traditional Christmas Eve dinners of Jeannie's childhood at the lodge: towers of crab legs, trays of oysters on beds of glistening shaved ice, hot lobster bisque, and sides of warm corn bread and shrimp toasts.

After dessert, there would be cards and nightcaps in the great room, then the groom would retire to a double suite, which would be cleaned in between the rehearsal dinner and wedding day for the sisters of the bride, while the bride would spend her last unmarried night having a slumber party with her sisters in what would be the bridal suite the next night.

Now Celeste had to think fast to find someone who would be able to fill in for her father at the last minute.

"Espresso?" she asked her mother, who was already rolling out dough for the next pastry, her irritation clear in her aggressive motions.

"I've already had two," Jeannie said. "I'm going to put these in the oven, then I'll warm up some soup for your father. And can you call Kristopsen's when they open? Our order was delayed yesterday. I want to make sure they're still doing a drop-off this morning."

"On it. Let me know if you need anything else," Celeste said, then took her coffee to the great room and blew on her drink while she stared out the window. The pale light of the rising sun was starting to creep up the tree line, a morning mist thick on the ground. It would burn off by eleven, and with the trees already budding ahead of schedule, it was going to be a gorgeous weekend for an early-spring wedding.

She took a small sip of her coffee. It was obvious who she needed to call. But what if he said no? What if he said yes? Celeste would have to basically be Jack's boss for the next couple of days and ensure that he offered her guests the bespoke experience the lodge had guaranteed.

There was also the small fact that Quinn would have a field day. Their father and his cover band had been a last-minute substitution on Christmas Eve so many years ago when the jazz trio had canceled and her parents' love story had begun. Celeste didn't want to endure her sister's matchmaking glee at the parallel turn of events.

There wasn't really a choice to be made. Jack could deliver, and it wasn't like there was much time to explore other options. It was her duty to make sure that the wedding weekend was as perfect as she could possibly make it, especially since over a million people would be witness to the event.

Without overthinking, she opened the Wallace Expeditions account on Instagram and sent Jack a DM: *"Any chance you're free to manage a group tomorrow? Something outdoorsy? 6 guys."* She put her phone down and paced around the room, making small adjustments to picture frames on the walls and fluffing pillows. Jack likely wouldn't be up for a few hours, so she'd have to be patient.

She snatched her phone off the table again when it vibrated only seconds later. On the home screen was a response from Jack. Her heart raced. *"Count me in,"* read his message. "Yes," she whispered.

"Can you come by the lodge this afternoon to discuss?" she typed. *"Noon?"*

Another message came through almost immediately: *"See you then."*

She dropped her phone onto the table, while her stomach did flip-flops. She loved problem-solving.

Her solutions, however, didn't usually involve the prospect of working side by side with incredibly handsome men.

THE MORNING FLEW by in a flurry of checkouts and room preparations. The wedding group was due to start arriving at one o'clock, and in the meantime, Celeste was doing a final check of the main spaces before her meeting with Jack.

"You've rearranged those books six times in the last five minutes," Quinn said. "Is someone nervous?"

Celeste stepped back from the stack of coffee-table books in front of the fireplace. "I'm just tidying up," she shot back. "You could help, you know. And you're not to be anywhere in the vicinity of this room this afternoon."

"What if I want to say hi to Jack?"

"Too bad. Go latch hook a rug."

"Very funny," Quinn said. She approached Celeste and straightened the collar on her green blouse. "But you don't need to be nervous. You're gorgeous, and Jack is totally into you."

"I don't need him to be into me; I need him to show the group a great time. And I'm not nervous."

Quinn was right—Celeste was nervous. And she was also incredibly stressed. Half of their order from Kristopsen's still hadn't been delivered, and the seafood dinner was starting to look a lot less like a feast and more like an afternoon snack. After going over some logistics with Jack, who would be there any minute, she had to call around to all the local providers to see who had any stock. Not to mention finishing prepping all the rooms, restocking the mini fridges with bottles of cava and bags of truffle-oil potato chips, as per the bride and groom's special request, and making sure that when everyone arrived, the lodge was ready to shine.

The chimes at the front door rang, indicating someone had just passed through, and Quinn gave Celeste a quick peck on the cheek. "I'll be in the kitchen if you need anything."

Celeste smoothed her hair and went to the front entrance, anticipation swirling like a whirlpool in her gut. Jack stood in the lobby in jeans, a black bomber jacket, and a baseball cap.

"Hey, Jack," she said.

"Hey. Wow," he said, glancing around at the lodge's entrance. "This place is incredible."

"Thanks," said Celeste. She basked in the glow of his approval, feeling the same rush of pride she experienced whenever a new guest entered the lodge. "Come on in." She motioned toward the great room, where the fire was crackling and the coffee-table books looked just right. "Can I get you something to drink? Tea or coffee?"

"I'll take a coffee," said Jack. "Black."

"Make yourself comfortable. I'll be right back."

Minutes later, when she reentered the great room balancing a tray with two coffees and a plate of white chocolate–dipped biscotti, she found Jack surveying the bookshelves, pulling out titles from the nature section. "I haven't seen these in years," he said, flipping through a volume of the *Life* Nature Library set.

"My parents are big collectors. Feel free to borrow one," she said.

"I remember reading these in grade school." He surveyed the rest of the shelf, where some of Everett's published books were also featured. "Where's the mystery section?"

Celeste smiled. "That's in the puzzle room. You like mysteries?"

Jack's eyes widened. "The puzzle room? You have an actual puzzle room?"

"We own a lot of puzzles—and even more mystery novels. I think we keep our Clue board game there too."

He grinned. "I love that."

Celeste loved how his eyes were alight with an infectious energy. She was tempted to ask him about his favorite authors, his opinion on the most deceptive red herring of all time, and what he thought about the television adaptation of the Three Pines series, but they had business to attend to. "I can give you the grand tour later. Here—have your coffee while it's still hot." She gestured toward the seating area in front of the fireplace.

Jack settled into one of the caramel leather couches, picked up his mug, and took a sip. "Great coffee. So, tell me about this group."

Celeste opened her iPad. "It's the groom, his best man—the other groomsman, the brother of the bride is arriving the morning of the wedding—another one of Jeff's friends, the fathers of the bride and groom, and the great-uncle of the bride. So, six altogether."

"And they were supposed to be doing what?"

"Outdoor adventure."

"What does that mean?"

"It means whatever my dad decides in the moment. It depends on a number of factors. Weather, season, recent wildlife sightings…"

"Sounds…adventurous," Jack said, a grin tugging at the corners of his lips. She liked his easygoing nature. It made her feel confident about turning over the tour to him.

"It's kinda what he's known for," said Celeste, her own smile mirroring his. "But now he's knocked out. So…"

"So that's where I come in. Do they know they're going fishing?"

"Not yet, but I'm sure they'll love it."

"Oh yeah? How do you know?"

"I don't. But I'm operating from a place of optimism."

"All right, given that I don't know their skill level, I'll plan for the classic workshop. Maybe you can give me a heads-up in the morning about approximate sizes. I'll get all the gear together, and we'll spend the day out on the Bow, get them pulling out some nice rainbow trout."

"What about lunch?" Celeste said.

"There's a burger joint at the river access that's pretty good. We can get a couple tables there when they're done."

"Hmm," Celeste said. With Everett's excursions, Jeannie would always send an elaborate picnic, and he had a number of places that were great to stop, rest, and enjoy a gourmet meal on the go. The diner was okay, but there was no guarantee there would be a table big enough for the group, and they didn't take reservations.

"You have another idea, it seems like."

"What if I bring by lunch? Is there somewhere we can set up?"

"Outside? I'm okay with that. But will your group be?"

"You know what? I'll take care of it. Just tell me what time and where." There were a couple of smaller portable heat lamps in the garage she could get Mariana, their head of housekeeping, to help her put into the back of the truck. "And your rate?"

"Four-fifty per guest for the half-day workshop," Jack said. "But I'll knock off 15 percent if you give my company a shout-out on your social media."

"Deal."

They spent a few more minutes covering logistics, and Celeste started to feel increasingly confident that this was going to be a good backup.

"Thanks again for this. I think it's going to be great," she said.

"You going to join us?" Jack said, a glint in his eye. "You're practically an expert at fly tying now."

"Uh-uh," Celeste said. "This is a guys' day. I'll be there to drop off lunch, but otherwise I'll be here, slinging mango margaritas and spinning Mariah Carey records."

Jack took the last gulp of his coffee and set his mug on the table. "So, how about that tour?"

"Right this way."

He followed her lead as she led him to her favorite spaces in the lodge. The sun was shining outside, so she took him to the artist's gallery. Jack was complimentary throughout the tour, noting small construction details and craftsmanship.

Celeste felt a mixture of pride tinged with sadness. This was supposed to be her forever home, and soon it would be in the hands of perfect strangers, and all of the things Jack was pointing out as being unique and memorable could be forever changed.

"And here," she said, stopping in the puzzle room, "is the final stop on today's tour. Which was the truncated version. I, unfortunately, have to source some red snapper for tomorrow's dinner."

"Why not serve rainbow trout?" Jack said. "It'll be fresh caught and much tastier than some imported, overrated catch. Plus the guys can show off the result of their work. I have a great recipe I can share with you. Super simple."

Celeste almost swooned. This was the second problem of hers that Jack had solved in a matter of hours. "You'd better be careful, or I'm going to have to hire you on staff," she said. "You're making yourself indispensable."

"I'm more of an outdoors guy. But it seems like a pretty great place to work."

She tried to smile, but a lump formed in her throat.

"Or not?" Jack said, studying her expression.

"No, it is. It's just that my parents are selling the place this summer. So, I'm going to start looking for somewhere new to work. Any interest in owning your very own lodge?" she joked, trying to deflect attention from the waver in her voice.

When she looked back at Jack, his expression had softened and his chocolate-brown eyes were filled with concern. "I'm sorry to hear that," he said. "But I'm sure whoever buys it will want to keep you on. You seem…" He paused, and Celeste was on pins and needles waiting for the rest of his response. He cleared his throat. "You're clearly good at your job."

Warmth filled Celeste from her feet to the end of her ponytail. "Thank you. So this," she said, motioning to the room, "is the puzzle room."

Jack took a few steps in, surveyed the room, and grinned. "This is awesome."

"Books are organized by subgenre. Police procedurals on that wall. Classics over there. Cozy mysteries beside the fireplace. Legal thrillers by the window, historicals beside that. And then it's classic noir, romantic suspense, and supernatural."

Jack laughed. "This is unbelievable!" He walked around the room, looking the shelves up and down. "You literally own every mystery novel ever published. Have you read them all?"

Celeste smiled. "Let's just say I have some creative ideas for where to hide a dead body."

"Noted," said Jack. He took a step closer to the classics shelf. "Is this…" He pulled a leather-bound book and looked at her, amazed.

"Yep. *Death on the Nile*, first edition."

She watched as Jack turned it over in his hands. "Agatha

Christie is my favorite of all time. My grams had every single one of her books and would read them to me way before it was ever age appropriate."

Grams? Celeste had to stifle a giggle at the sound of such an adorable term of endearment coming from a rugged outdoorsman.

"My dad bought it at auction, like, twenty years ago for what he thought at the time was a small fortune. But I think it was a good investment," she said.

"I'll say. But wait, so you just keep these out here? Where anyone could take them?"

"We've been lucky. Our guests are pretty awesome." If Jack looked a little more closely, he'd see that there was also a camera surveillance system in most of the common rooms. They really only used it so that whoever was at the front desk could see when there were guests using the spaces so staff could offer them service, but she supposed it would also be helpful in the event of a book heist.

"I'm sure they're distracted by biscotti. Those were amazing."

Celeste smiled. "I'll let my mom know." She was tempted to linger in the puzzle room with Jack and continue comparing notes on their favorite books. She could picture it: Them sitting in front of the fire together reading. Without thinking, she'd move her feet into his lap, and he'd hold them, and she'd love it. Eventually she'd notice that he wasn't reading anymore and that he was looking at her in a way that told her *they* weren't reading anymore. And she'd dog-ear her book—which was a cardinal sin, in her opinion—but she wouldn't care, and soon they'd be wishing for the fire to die down with the heat generated by their two bodies, naked in front of the hearth.

Her cheeks burned when she realized Jack had just said something, but she was caught in the trance of a sexy reading dream. "I'm sorry?" she said, hoping her cheeks weren't as cherry red as they felt.

"I asked which one is your favorite."

"Contemporary? I'm a huge Ann Cleeves fan. And of the classics…I've never met an Ian Fleming I didn't like."

"Bond fan, eh?"

"I like Bond." She had a million things on her to-do list, but suddenly they seemed as pressing as organizing the paperclips in the office. She liked talking to Jack. A lot. She also liked the way his lips smile curved a little more on the right and how he looked at her like she was the most interesting person in the world. "Do you know he also wrote *Chitty Chitty Bang Bang*?"

"I did not," Jack said. He looked at his watch. "But speaking of flying cars, I might need one of my own if I'm going to make it to the tackle shop in time to grab a few things I need for tomorrow."

"I'll walk you out," Celeste said.

They moved to the foyer. "Thanks again for helping us out tomorrow," she said. "You're a lifesaver."

"Pleasure's all mine. I'll be by with the van at eight thirty sharp."

"See you then," Celeste said, already counting down the hours. "Don't forget to send me the invoice."

"Will do. And by the way," Jack said, turning around on his way back to his truck, "Tiffany Case. That's your Bond character."

Celeste laughed. "What? You're comparing me to a diamond smuggler?"

"You've got a great sense of humor," he said, his eyes flickering with amusement and something that, if Celeste wasn't mistaken, looked a lot like desire. "And...you seem like you're not opposed to diamonds."

She twisted the ring on her right middle finger. It was a replica of Princess Diana's ring that her parents had given her for her thirtieth birthday, a large blue sapphire surrounded by a ring of diamonds. "You're not wrong about that," Celeste said. Was he judging her? By the looks of it, the only diamonds that interested Jack were the black-diamond runs on the nearby mountains. She watched as he descended the front steps of the lodge. "Bye, Jack."

Jack turned back and gave her a quick wave, then got into his truck. As he pulled out, he honked twice.

Celeste went back into the lodge, closed the door, and leaned against it. When had she ever been this swoony? She shook her head. Jack was now pretty much a colleague, who was doing this to help his business, not to help her.

She watched as his truck disappeared around the forested bend, then sighed.

It was official—she was hot for teacher.

Chapter Seven

THE THICK MORNING mist was starting to burn off when Jack pulled back into the lodge's parking lot a few minutes before the agreed-upon time. The forecast for the day was cool but clear, and he'd gotten some intel from Hank at the tackle shop about a few spots where some trout were holding, so chances were good they'd get some catches.

He got out of his truck just as Celeste exited the front door holding her clipboard in one hand and waving at him with the other. "Hey!" she called. "They're all just finishing up breakfast. Everyone's excited. You want a coffee?"

Her warm welcome cut right through the cold air and early-morning fog. "Nah, I'm good—thanks," Jack said. "Picked one up at Ronnie's."

"I'll pack a pasty for you, then. You haven't lived until you've had a Jeannie McCarthy jalapeño-sundried tomato scone."

"Sounds great." He approached the porch and took a moment to appreciate the slim fit of her gray knit dress and the way her glossy hair spilled over her shoulders. It wasn't much past the crack of dawn, and the way she looked like she was stepping out of a fashion magazine had him perking up more than any coffee ever could. "So, what time do I need to have these guys back here?" he asked. "It's going to be a beauty of a day."

Celeste consulted her notes. "Dinner is at seven, so if you can have them back by five thirty, six, that should give everyone enough time to shower and have a few minutes to regroup." She looked up. "Oh, and Jack?"

"Yeah?"

"The bride has issued strict instructions that under no circumstances should these men be allowed to drink today."

"You mean alcohol?"

"I mean alcohol."

Jack blinked. "This is a bachelor party, isn't it?"

"The bachelor party was in Nashville. This is a 'groom's day out.'"

"So, it's basically a daytime bachelor party." While it was a bylaw infraction to drink in a national park, Jack turned a blind eye to the occasional tall can or bottle, as long as everyone took care of their garbage.

"Groom's day out." Celeste gave him a stern expression. He liked being told what to do by her. He just hoped she didn't really expect him to listen. There was no chance he was searching bags or giving a predeparture lecture to a group of grown men.

"There's nothing wrong with a can of beer or something on break, is there? I mean, I don't supply anything, but—"

"No." Celeste pursed her lips and looked behind her. "I'm not kidding. Kassie's a little...particular," she whispered.

"Is that code for *tight-ass*?"

Celeste looked over her shoulder again. "Shh," she said, laughing a little. "It's code for *don't let it happen*. I was in some of the rooms yesterday for turndown service, and the best man seems to have brought an entire bar cart's worth of liquor on this trip. And Jeff gave all the guys inscribed stainless-steel flasks as gifts. So, you need to keep an eye on things."

Jack opened his mouth to shoot back something at Celeste. As much as he didn't like her setting parameters for how to run his business, the McCarthys were paying him for this last-minute booking, and he was in no position to be difficult. "All right," he said. "I'll keep things dry on the river."

"Promise?"

He grinned, enjoying the expectant expression on her face. Clearly she ran a tight ship at the lodge, and this was her MO. "Promise."

Celeste appeared satisfied. The door opened behind her, and she moved aside as one by one, the groom and his best man, another friend, the fathers of the bride and groom, and a lanky old man with a goatee and a ballcap on who introduced himself as Uncle Jasper, filtered outside.

"There they are!" Celeste exclaimed with a tone change

that was clearly practiced but still genuine. "Everyone had enough to eat?"

Uncle Jasper patted his belly. "Your mother is a sweet angel from heaven," he said. He looked at Jack. "You the guide? I'm known for my trick casts, but I'm a drowning risk today after those cinnamon buns. I hope you have good insurance. Or maybe I'll just go to bed so I can wake up in the morning and experience that all over again."

"We're happy to deliver them directly to your room tomorrow morning, if you'd like," Celeste said.

Jasper opened his arms and looked up at the sky. "Thank you, Lord, for bringing me to this place!" he exclaimed.

Jack grinned, then turned to the group. "All right. Who's ready to bring home tonight's dinner?"

AN HOUR LATER, the group of six were outfitted, given a quick lesson on casting and how to wade safely, and were standing out in the gentle currents of the Bow River awaiting their next instructions. Jack demoed what he'd shown them on land again in the water and watched and gave small corrections as they tried their hands at their first casts.

"Fly-fishing is a two-handed sport," he said. "Cast with your right hand and use your left hand for line management. I want everyone to check the drag on your reel. If it's turned off and loose all the way and you pull line, it's going to overspool and you'll be dealing with a bird's nest."

The group caught on pretty quickly, and Uncle Jasper hadn't been kidding when he'd bragged about being an expert at trick casts. Jack did an internal *hell yeah* when a bald eagle swooped down to the river right where the group was practicing casting and snatched a whitefish right out of the water, causing a raucous cheer to erupt at the creature's majesty and dominance.

As predicted, the weather was stunning, and while Jack did catch a glimpse or two of the sparkle of a flask tipping back in the sun, everyone seemed to be behaving themselves. Celeste didn't need to know. It was a guys' day out, for goodness' sake.

The guys were having fun, joking around, and Jack felt confident that the day was already a success.

Around noon, about an hour before Celeste was scheduled to arrive with lunch, Jeff sloshed through the river to where Jack was standing. "Hey, Jack, how much you wanna bet I'm going home with the biggest catch today?" he said.

Jack squinted. Now that he was paying attention, Jeff's speech might've been slurring just the teensiest bit. He'd have to do a better job at keeping their hands full.

"I'll tell you what," Jack said, passing Jeff his rod. "If you hold these two rods and manage to keep the casts from tangling for at least two minutes, I'll give you twenty bucks."

The groom laughed. "A challenge! All right fellas, come on over and witness greatness!"

Two minutes later, Jack was down twenty bucks but the group was very much into the idea of contests and betting, and a simple introductory workshop had morphed into a series of made-up competitions and feats of physical endurance, including a sprint race through the river with waders on that Jack was mildly concerned would end in someone falling and getting their clothing soaking wet (he had some extras in the truck) and a longest-cast contest. Uncle Jasper introduced them to an old challenge that involved trying to cast to flick a cigarette out of someone's mouth, and when Jasper put a cigarette between his lips and the guys started egging Jack on, he caved and gave it a shot, succeeding in one go.

It was actually pretty fun, although he had to shut down a couple of unsafe ideas, especially given the fact that there might have been some tippling involved. He could play dumb about that to Celeste, but an accident or injury would be less forgivable.

He'd thought the contests had distracted them, but when the best man, Kurt, tried to convince the group to shed their gear and skinny-dip, touting the benefits of a cold plunge, Jack knew he was in trouble.

"Nah, we're going to keep our clothes on, gents," he said. "You guys ever seen *Stand By Me*? You think those leeches were big, you haven't seen anything yet."

It was a bald-faced lie, but it seemed to do the trick, and the comment was met with boisterous laughter from the group.

Jeff came over and patted him on the back. "You're the best, man," he said. The whiff of whiskey on Jeff's breath left him with no question that the groom would soon be three sheets to the wind.

Jack took a deep breath in. He'd for sure be in the doghouse with Celeste, but some food was exactly what this group needed.

"All right," he called. "Who's ready for lunch?"

IT WAS SHORTLY after one when Celeste pulled into the forest clearing where they'd arranged to meet. There wasn't a soul to be seen, but she was early and wanted to get all set up before the group arrived back from their session.

The sun shone bright overhead as Celeste pulled the catering trays from the back of the van, then wheeled the lamps over to the picnic tables.

The meal was simple but hearty: a tray of boeuf bourguignon, with a chickpea stew for the vegetarian, roasted vegetables and garlic potatoes, Jeannie's famous brussels sprout coleslaw, and homemade root beer from Best Case Brewery in town. She'd packed the remaining loaves of sourdough bread and butter from breakfast, and the cherry cheesecake she lugged out of the back of the van must have weighed twenty pounds.

Once everything was set up, Celeste perched on the picnic table, scrolling through her phone as she waited.

She heard before she saw them: male voices loudly singing "Home for a Rest" rang clear through the air. When she looked up from her phone, she saw the crew of them wading through the riverbanks toward her, gesticulating and marching in a way that was decidedly…festive.

He didn't.

One by one, the fishers emerged from the river toward her, some walking in a staggered fashion that couldn't be wholly attributed to the uneven ground.

She was going to kill Jack.

Her blood started to boil. "There she is! Madame Butterfly!" Kurt exclaimed, arms raised, his bucket hat askew. "We come bearing gifts!"

Jeff and the his dad, walking side by side with their arms around each other's shoulders, were now chanting something that Celeste guessed was a sports team cheer of some kind. Jeff held a cooler, which he extended to her as they approached. "Here! Dinner for tonight!" he said. He stopped and surveyed the immaculately laid out picnic tables. Celeste suddenly regretted the white tablecloths. She'd have been smarter to bring plastic bibs.

Jack was at the back of the group, holding another cooler and a net, and looking at her sheepishly. He appeared to be sober, a fact that was keeping her from spearing him with one of his fishing rods.

"I'm sorry," he said quietly when he was right next to her. "They had flasks in their backpacks. I couldn't stop them."

Celeste faked a wide grin for the benefit of the guests, who were circling the picnic table. One of them made no attempt to hide another deep tip of his flask. "Kassie is going to kill me," she hissed. Not only that, but she was also going to give the lodge a terrible review on her social media, and the Keystone Ridge Resort was going to see that rating, and Celeste was 100 percent going to be out of the running for the management job.

"Let's get them some food, sober them up, then I'll take them back out for a bit. They'll be totally fine by the time we get back to the lodge," Jack said, his eyes pleading.

Celeste clenched her jaw. "All right, everyone!" she said, doing her best to project a tone of jovial merriment. "Time to eat!"

Amazingly, the party were able to serve themselves, although the tablecloth would likely have to be discarded there was so much spillage.

Celeste poured root beers, which were tasty enough to distract the group from substituting with more alcohol and made sure their cups stayed full in hopes that they'd rehydrate a bit. After twenty minutes, she was able to sit down and rest for a moment while the group enjoyed their lunch.

"I'm really sorry," Jack said, joining her at the empty picnic table with a plate. "Honestly. I think sometimes these things just take on a life of their own. And…at the end of the day, it's pretty tame for a bachelor party. Groom's day out, I mean."

"I get it," Celeste said. It was also Jeff's wedding, and if this was something that made the weekend more special for him, she had to respect that. Even if it came at the cost of her plans to salvage her career.

When she looked over at Jack, he had a funny look on his face. He chewed and swallowed, then looked at her intently. "This," he said, "is the most unbelievable field meal I've ever tasted."

"You can tell that to Jeannie," she said.

"And the guys are clearly happy."

Celeste looked over at the other picnic table. "Jeff Grant likes to appear low maintenance—a 'down-to-earth guy's guy.' But he likes the finer things in life."

"What? How do you know?"

"Well, firstly, he gets highlights. That baby-soft skin is the product of a monthly facial. He's wearing a Comme des Garçons T-shirt under that fleece, and when I mentioned the word *bespoke* attached to this expedition, he nearly fell over swooning. I know his type. This was not a cellophane-wrapped-sandwich kind of day."

"Huh," Jack said, a funny look in his eyes. "You're perceptive, that's for sure. Now I'm feeling all self-conscious. You're going to figure out all my secrets."

Celeste grinned. "I had you all figured out two minutes

after walking into your classroom." Which wasn't true, not in the slightest. Jack had already surprised her on more than one occasion.

"Well, whatever that superpower is, it's working. These guys haven't shut up all day, and yet I haven't heard a peep out of them since they started eating."

"Happy to be of service."

Jack took another bite of his meal. "I should start serving this every day," he said. "People will sign up just for the lunch." He wiped his mouth with the napkin. "I mean, the cloth napkins might be a little over the top."

Celeste raised an eyebrow. "Nothing wrong with a little elegance. Who doesn't love being pampered?"

"Speaking of elegance…" Jack said, looking over at Kurt, who had his back to them but was clearly peeing into the river.

Celeste's jaw dropped, then she buried her head in her arm on the table. "Gross. Oh my goodness," she said, stifling a giggle and turning to look the other way. "Is this how people behave on your tours? You need to institute a code of conduct."

"And you need to institute a practice of searching bags for Crown Royal," Jack said. He took another bite of his stew. "Seriously. I need this recipe."

Celeste smiled. "I'll pack you whatever's left over."

She spent the next thirty minutes encouraging the group to grab seconds, topping off their root beers with what was left, then, with Jack's help, packing up the catering bins and loading her truck, then bidding the group farewell as they departed for the remainder of the afternoon. Jack had (wisely, in Celeste's opinion) gauged that the group wasn't going to do much more in the way of productive fishing and had decided to tour them around in the drift boat in the bay near the Thompson Marina for another hour and show them the sights, then get them back to the lodge slightly earlier than originally planned, in time to nap off the alcohol before that night's rehearsal dinner.

There was a moment working with Jack that she'd felt like they were a team, a partnership. Like she could confide in him, trust him. Working all these years for her parents, she'd never experienced that before. She'd always felt like, well, their kid. And the idea of being on someone's level, working toward a shared goal—it had felt good. Really good.

But the last thing she needed at this point in her life was to latch on to something else that she'd only stand to lose.

IT WAS LATE afternoon when Celeste returned to the lodge. The sun was big and hazy in the sky, and when she entered through the back, she found her mother pulling a rack of gougères from the oven. "Hi, honey," Jeannie said. "How'd it go?"

Celeste was about to answer but was interrupted by peals

of laughter coming from the great room. "Good. Sounds like all's well here?"

Jeannie raised an eyebrow. "Something tells me it'll be early to bed tonight."

"Well, whatever state Jeff and company return in, they'll be absolved."

As suspected, when Celeste poked her head into the great room, there were empty cocktail coupes and open bottles of Laurent-Perrier amid the table of cupcakes and macarons on the table. It was the bride's mother, Victoria, whose eyes were the glossiest, and no wonder—she looked to be about ninety pounds soaking wet.

No one noticed Celeste, so she quietly passed through the hallway back to the kitchen, where Mariana was helping Jeannie putting the finishing touches on the tiered seafood tower. She passed her mother the cooler of rainbow trout.

"The snapper arrived while you were gone," Jeannie said. "We can freeze these. Everything's almost done. What time will they be back?"

"Jack took them out for another hour or so to sober up," Celeste said. She put her finger up to her lips. "Shh."

Jeannie smiled and shook her head. "Well, at least no one drowned," she said.

"Don't jinx us," said Celeste, rapping on the wood countertop. "How's Dad?"

"Still has a bit of a fever. He's sleeping. I'm trying not to go too close. The last thing we need is for the rest of us to get sick."

"Agreed," said Celeste.

"So, this guide," said Jeannie. She soaped up her hands and started rubbing them vigorously under the running water. "He's good? Maybe he can be our new backup."

Celeste passed her mother a tea towel. "It seems to have worked out," she said, trying to hide her enthusiasm.

"Well, thanks for arranging that so last minute. He was a real lifesaver."

Celeste couldn't disagree with that. "I'll go check and see if anyone needs anything in the great room," she said.

As she moved between the kitchen and the great room, where the chatter and laughter was still alive and well, Celeste's phone buzzed in her back pocket. *We're heading back. See you soon. Everyone on best behavior*," read the message.

Celeste smiled to herself. "*10-4*," she replied. She stopped in the bathroom next to the office to check her hair in case Jack decided to come in. She let out a sigh of both exasperation and something else—excitement? She didn't *want* to want Jack to come in. She didn't want to loiter near the door in case he was simply planning to drop off the group, then continue on with his day, so that she could pop her head out and thank him in person before he took off. But here she was.

She wanted it.

She wanted him.

Chapter Eight

THE DRIVE BACK to the lodge was more civilized than Jack had anticipated it might be only a few hours earlier. The group was still lively and animated, but the jovial shouting had faded to indoor voices, curse words were no longer flowing as easy as the Bow River, and Jack was no longer worried that Celeste was going to have his neck.

He grinned to himself, picturing the fiery expression in her eyes and the way she pursed her glossy lips. She'd been so deliciously annoyed, he'd wanted to pick her up right there and kiss those lips, temper that annoyance, and distract her with another feeling. He longed to give her that other feeling.

"Cap!" called Jeff from the back seat. They'd started calling him Captain soon after they'd gotten back out on the water after lunch and had grilled him about his travels. They'd been enthralled with his stories of falling down a fifteen-foot waterfall in Brazil, and he'd had them in stitches when telling them about the time he'd camped out in the open air in the desert near Joshua Tree and woken up covered from head to toe with fire ants.

"Yes, my man," said Jack, navigating into the Butterfly Lake Lodge parking lot.

"What are you doing now? Want to come in for the rehearsal dinner?"

Jack grimaced. There wasn't much more he hated in the world than weddings or wedding-adjacent events. He hated dressing up. He hated sitting through syrupy-sweet speeches. He hated celebrating couples he knew were all wrong, who likely wouldn't make it more than five years, and being forced to toast them over and over again throughout the course of the evening over rubbery chicken and limp vegetables.

Christine had convinced him that their wedding would be different—they'd have a simple ceremony in the Cascade Garden in Banff, then a casual dinner with close friends and family at Herbie's, their favorite restaurant just outside of town with an outdoor patio overlooking the mountains.

He'd relented. He'd been wrapped around Christine's little finger for most things. The woman was a practiced pouter and a master of manipulation. She'd left him in the dust anyway, before he'd even had the chance to buy her a ring. At least he could be thankful for that.

No way did he want to go to a wedding rehearsal dinner, especially for someone he'd only known for a matter of hours.

"Ah, no can do," Jack said. "Thanks for the invitation, though. You sure picked a good spot to get married." He brought the van to a stop in the spot right beside the lodge's front steps, just as the front door opened and Celeste appeared, clipboard in hand again and the door open in the other to welcome back her guests. She'd changed again since she'd brought lunch, from her jeans and pullover back into the form-fitting gray knit dress she was wearing earlier that morning, her hair loose around her shoulders. It was a good thing he was wearing sunglasses and she couldn't see his expression fixed like a powerful magnet on her stunning figure. She was a total knockout.

He gave her a quick wave through the windshield as the groom and his party started to unload from the van, thanking and praising him, promising to look him up next time they were in the area and to pass on the name of his company to friends.

He got out of the car. Uncle Jasper shook his hand, and Jeff clapped him on his shoulder. "Seriously Captain, we'd love to have you come tonight! If your plans change, come on by." He looked up at Celeste. "No problem adding one more, right?"

She smiled. "Of course not."

"This guy's a legend," said Kurt. He gave Jack another fist bump, then disappeared into the lodge, leaving Celeste and Jack alone on the porch.

"Wow," she said. "Seems like you made quite the impression."

"They were a fun group," he said.

"Luckily not too much fun," Celeste said. There was a pause, and Jack wondered if he needed to apologize again. "So, are you going to come?" she said. "For dinner?"

"I doubt he was serious," he said. "And I'd be willing to bet that if I looked at that clipboard of yours, an extra guest might get in the way of some carefully crafted plans. Plus I don't do weddings."

"What, you don't like good music, great food, and happiness?"

Was she trying to convince him to stay? "Ha," he said. "I like all those things. But without the side of cheesiness and that wedding cake with the chewy, hard icing. What's wrong with buttercream?"

"It's called fondant. Also, clearly you've never been to a Butterfly Lake Lodge wedding," Celeste said. "We do it right. Cream-cheese frosting all the way. And if we do buttercream, it's Swiss meringue."

He had no idea what she was talking about, but the way she said it gave him do doubt whatever kind of frosting it was would be as sweet as the lips that formed those words. "You're making me hungry again," Jack said. "If that lunch today was any indication of what's coming their way, you're going to have some happy wedding guests."

"That's the plan," Celeste said. "You know, it might be considered good customer service to accept that invite."

He raised an eyebrow. "That would really be going above and beyond."

Celeste shrugged. "That's what customer service is, isn't it? Just saying."

She was leaving the door wide open for him, and he was happy to walk right on through. "I don't have a date," Jack said. "Know any beautiful clipboard-toting brunettes in the area who might be free tonight?"

Celeste grinned, and he lapped up the playful expression in her emerald green eyes. "Tonight I might have my hands full." She glanced at her watch. "I should probably go in."

He was almost tempted to join her, but he knew what that might lead to. He might actually have a really good time. And he might be tempted to call her again to see if she wanted to have dinner somewhere just the two of them, somewhere dim and kind of quiet, where he could sit across from her for hours and talk about real things, not just the businesses they were running but the things they did after-hours. What made her tick. What she wanted in life. What made her feel good. All the things that would mean he was sliding right back into his old patterns.

They were standing close enough to touch and far enough away from the window that no one would be able to see them. Knowing they had a moment of privacy embold-ened Jack to reach out and take Celeste's hand in his. She didn't pull away. "Well, maybe another time then," he said.

Her chin tipped up slightly, and without thinking, he moved even closer, looking for the permission he needed to kiss her.

But it was Celeste who made the first move, and as soon as her soft lips met his and the flowery smell of her flooded over him, he was a goner. With one hand holding hers and the other moving to the small of her back, he moved his lips hungrily over Celeste's, reveling in the sweet taste of her, the warm smoothness of her skin that brushed against his cheek, the feeling of her breath.

She pulled back slightly, her eyes heavy with desire, her chest rising and falling. "I need to get inside," she whispered. She leaned in and kissed him again. He would take as much as she could get. When she pulled back a second time, she lay a hand on his chest, further stoking the flame of desire.

As much as it pained him to rip himself away from Celeste, she had a job to do, and it was best to make his way home before he slid any further down this tunnel. If there was any doubt that Celeste had the power to completely undo him, it had vanished under the power of kissing her.

"All right, well, I'd better hit the road," Jack said, his voice hoarse. For a second, he reconsidered staying for dinner, just to get more time with Celeste, but not only did he know she was busy hosting, there was a nagging feeling in his chest that indulging in this flirtation was leading him in a direction he knew he couldn't go.

Celeste nodded, and he detected a flash of disappointment in her expression. "Thanks again for everything today," she said. "See you in class on Monday?"

Right. Class. He'd see her again on Monday and maybe

around town, but this business of whatever was hanging thick in the air between them, it needed cooling off. "Last class," Jack said. "We're doing a Jock Scott. Pack your patience. It's a tricky one."

"Ohh," said Celeste. "The moment I've been waiting for." She glanced over her shoulder. "I'd better go," she said, her voice all smoky and caramel. "Take care, Jack."

"Good luck tonight and tomorrow," he said, descending the steps back to his truck, the magnetic pull of her fighting to keep him from leaving. "Oh, and watch out for that Kurt character," Jack said. "He seemed to have taken a liking to you. Wouldn't shut up about it out on the water, actually." He liked Kurt. But the idea of him making any kind of move on Celeste made him picture clocking the guy.

"Is that right?" said Celeste. "Well, don't worry about me. I can hold my own." Her sly smile just about made his knees buckle.

"I don't doubt it," said Jack, sliding into the driver's seat of his van. He didn't doubt it one bit. "G' night, Celeste."

A FEW MINUTES after midnight, Celeste dropped her clipboard onto the desk in the office. Her eyelids were heavy and her body buzzed with the exertion of the day, and she was considering just tumbling into bed in her dress with her makeup still on.

She was dying to sleep, but there was a good chance she'd be up, wide awake, with finally a moment to process what had happened on the porch earlier with Jack.

In the darkness of the office, she closed her eyes for a moment, recalling the involuntary reaction the moment he'd been close, close enough to see the dark flecks in his brown eyes, to hear his shallow breath and see the rise and fall of his chest. It wasn't just his proximity that had stirred her senses. It was the certainty that he'd wanted exactly what she had, only she hadn't hesitated. Kissing Jack hadn't been a decision. It had been a fully instinctual urge, and when her lips had found his, that same drive had allowed her to silence any thought that she was making a mistake.

Each brush of Jack's lips, coupled with the firmness of his hands as he'd pulled her close, had sent shivers tingling down her spine, and the rumbling grunt of pleasure that had escaped his mouth when she'd pulled back had been almost enough to make her ditch the rehearsal party and let them fend for themselves for the night.

The swiftness of the goodbye and the quick reentry to the bright lights of the lodge had made it seem like a dream. Kissing Jack had been surreal. And that image, burned in her brain, the feeling of him imprinted on her skin—no amount of exhaustion was going to keep that off her mind when she lay her head on the pillow.

She flicked the office light off. The lodge was quiet, and it seemed as though everyone was in bed, getting some sleep before what would be a big day.

The groom and his buddies had stayed up a little later than everyone else, playing poker in the great room, so Celeste went to check that there weren't any glasses left behind, pillows astray, or books needing straightening.

Without turning on the light, she moved through the dim room to the cards table, which was lit up by moonlight, and picked up a beer bottle and two rocks glasses.

The sound of a gentle whimper made her start. "Hello?" Celeste said, scanning the room.

"Sorry," came a quiet voice, barely audible from the puzzle room. "I didn't mean to scare you."

Celeste deposited the glasses back onto the table, then flicked on the standing Tiffany lamp beside the couch. Curled up in a big leather chair, in her hot-pink pajamas and fluffy slippers, was the bride, clutching a tissue, her deep brown eyes filled with tears.

"Kassie?" Celeste said. "Is everything okay?"

Kassie sniffed, then wiped her nose with the sleeve of her pajama shirt. "I'm okay. Just nervous," she said. She rolled her big, lashy eyes, which filled again with tears. "I know— so pathetic, right?"

Celeste perched on the arm of the other armchair that was facing Kassie. "I don't think that at all. Did something happen?" For a moment, a scene flashed in her mind of her having to tell the groom and the rest of the guests that the wedding was off. Canceling the catering. Figuring out what to do with over eight thousand dollars' worth of anemones, dahlias and sweet pea.

This needed delicate handling, and Kassie didn't seem like the type who needed too soft of a shoulder to cry on.

"No. I just…" She stopped and blew her nose, a far louder honk than Celeste had expected coming from such a slight person. Celeste scanned the room and retrieved another tissue box. "Thanks," Kassie said, pulling five out and laying them neatly on her lap. "Jeff is perfect. I love him so much, and I know he loves me."

Celeste waited. Jeff's devotion clearly wasn't the reason for Kassie's tears.

"It's just that my parents got divorced when I was little, and I saw what it did to them, and I just keep thinking—" She stopped again and dipped her head down, her shoulders shaking silently.

"You're worried that even though things are great now, they won't always be," Celeste said quietly.

Kassie nodded.

"I get it," Celeste said. She paused. "I think that no one can ever predict what will happen five years, ten years, fifty years down the line. But you've seen what can happen when a relationship isn't properly tended to. And something tells me you'll keep that in mind for your own marriage."

"Yeah," Kassie said. She wiped her nose with the tissue.

"I think it's a leap of faith. And you're making it with all the right intentions and with all your heart. It's clear you really love Jeff. And I've seen how he looks at you."

Kassie took a deep shaky breath. "He's obsessed with me. Like, in a good way. I'm his queen."

Celeste nodded vigorously. "You totally are. You're his queen. And I think you two have many, many years of happiness ahead of you."

A small smile spread across Kassie's lips. "Thank you," she said. "I think so too."

"Now, no more crying," Celeste said. "You don't want puffy eyes tomorrow. But I'll make sure we have some cucumber slices in the fridge just in case. Come on," she said and extended her hand. Kassie allowed Celeste to pull her up, and before she could move, Kassie engulfed her in a surprisingly bone-breaking hug.

"Thank you again. I'm going to bed." She picked up her tissues and straightened her pink silk robe.

"Just call if you need anything," Celeste said. "Good night, Kassie."

Kassie's vulnerability had surprised her, but the woman truly was a queen, and she'd be perched high on her social media throne tomorrow—that was for sure.

Kassie disappeared upstairs, and Celeste cleared the tissues and glasses and bottle, sliced up some emergency cucumbers and placed them in a bowl in the fridge, then glanced at the clock in the kitchen—one o'clock.

Leap of faith?

She closed her eyes, remembering the sensation of Jack's

fingers tracing the sensitive skin at the back of her neck as he'd kissed her. He was a gorgeous man. And not only that but he was also a really good one too. Maybe she needed to take her own advice.

Chapter Nine

Harris/Grant Wedding Day Rundown

Morning:

- *6:30 a.m.: Begin prep coffee/mimosa/cinnamon bun trays for room delivery x 14 rooms (+ floral arrangement on bridal suite & MOB tray)*
- *7:30 a.m.: Floral delivery due (note—bouquets/boutonnieres to back fridge, calla lily arrangements to gallery for brunch tables, all others on fold-outs in kitchen—make sure to request emailed invoice)*
- *8:00 a.m.: Tray deliveries to rooms, check brunch setup in gallery *signs out for GF/DF*
- *9:00 a.m.: Extra coffee/tea/pastries in great room (bride provided playlist for ambient music through lodge—cued up on Spotify)*
- *10:00 a.m.: Brunch*

In the quiet of her kitchen, before heading to the lodge, Celeste clipped the four individual lists onto her clipboard, one for each segment of the day: morning, wedding prep,

ceremony/reception, and takedown. She always kept itinerar-
ies in sections, on separate pages. One thing at a time.
Having individual lists for each part of the day as its own
compartment kept things from getting overwhelming.

The entirety of the itinerary for the wedding day was
busy but manageable, and it all came down to having a
detailed plan, with every minute carefully thought through
in advance. Brunch would be served in the gallery, followed
by optional activities: a local artist was coming to lead a
watercolor lesson, Quinn was stepping in for Everett (who
wasn't running much of a fever anymore but was still
fatigued and, according to Jeannie, acting like a real grump)
to lead a hike around the periphery of Butterfly Lake, and
Jeannie would keep the snacks and drinks flowing for anyone
who just wanted to curl up with a book in front of the
fireplace in the great room.

The bridal party would be getting ready in their separate
spaces from about two o'clock on, ready for a sunset ceremony around six. Following that, it was cocktail hour and
then dinner.

It was dark, cold, and quiet when Celeste left her cabin
in the morning, desperate for coffee and bracing herself for a
jam-packed day with hopefully minimal surprises. She
stepped quickly down the path between her house and the
lodge. The caffeine was necessary, but the crisp morning air
was doing its job in jolting her awake.

Jeannie was sitting at the table with a coffee of her own

when Celeste entered the kitchen. "G' morning, Mom," she said and kissed her on the cheek.

"You were up late last night," Jeannie said. "I noticed your porch light was still on at midnight when I went to bed."

"Bride issues. Crisis averted, though, I think," she said and filled her insulated travel mug up with coffee from the carafe. She only had time to drink it over the course of the morning, so keeping it warm was essential.

"Oh dear," said Jeannie. "Well, they're already up. Victoria called down to ask for the forecast."

"Don't they have a weather app?"

She shrugged. "I guess they think we have special intel."

"And?"

"Cloudy this morning but should clear up by noon."

"Perfect," Celeste said and took a sip of her coffee. With any luck, the backdrop to the wedding photos would be the perfect orangey light of the setting sun. Happy bride and groom. Smiles and goodwill...and all the likes on social media.

An hour later, Mariana had already delivered most of the trays for the second and third floors, but Celeste wanted to deliver to the bridal suite herself.

She was about to tap lightly on the door but pulled back when she heard heated voices on the other side of the door. She stood balancing her tray of warm cinnamon buns, a small carafe of brewed coffee, a pitcher of freshly squeezed juice and chilled champagne for mimosas, and a vase with a small bud arrangement picked from Everett's greenhouse.

"He couldn't even get it together to make it on time for his own sister's wedding!" she heard Kassie wail. "He hates that I'm getting all the attention. And now he's trying to ruin our day."

Celeste grimaced. This sounded like a problem that not even cinnamon buns were likely to fix.

"There's no way he did it on purpose," her sister said. "He picked a stupid flight time, given how often he has to work overtime. But Kevin wouldn't do this to hurt you."

This was definitely not good. Kevin, the youngest sibling in the Harris family, was the only wedding guest who hadn't yet arrived and was scheduled to land at the Calgary airport at noon and then be at the lodge by two p.m. at the latest, with lots of time to shower and get dressed. Celeste knew from Victoria and Gary that Kevin was a paramedic in Toronto, so maybe he was stuck at the scene of an accident or something. Something told Celeste that someone else's emergency, however, did not trump Kassie's wedding plans.

Balancing the tray, Celeste glanced at her watch. The wedding was only ten hours away. If Kevin could rebook on a flight out of Pearson Airport in the next hour or so, he might make it, but it wasn't looking good.

She put on her best optimistic face and rapped on the door. Maybe some sugar and cinnamon would diffuse the tension at least a bit.

"Come in," she heard.

She entered the room to find Kassie still in bed, the covers pulled up to her chest and under-eye patches framing her deadly gaze. The sisters, Melissa and Siena, were also wearing their matching monogrammed pajamas, the bright pink a stark contrast to the decidedly dark mood in the air.

"Happy wedding day, Kassie!" Celeste said, smiling widely and feigning innocence. "How did everyone sleep?" She scanned the room for a free space to deposit the tray, but every square inch was covered in makeup, hair products, iPads and phones and gift bags. "I brought you all something to snack on before brunch."

Siena, the youngest of the sisters, moved her feet off the coffee table so Celeste could set the tray down. "Thank you," she said, giving Celeste a look that translated to *We might need more than one bottle.* They could have as many bottles as they wanted after the ceremony, but Celeste was keeping everything stashed until then. No need for any more unnecessary drama.

"We're a groomsman down. Apparently it's freezing rain in Toronto and they've canceled most of the flights. And now the photos are ruined," Kassie said.

Celeste silently wondered to herself if Kassie was at all concerned with her brother's well-being, but she was going to go ahead and keep that thought to herself.

"The photos are going to be stunning," Melissa said. "And we can take some more pictures after Kevin gets here."

"But not at the wedding! I'm not getting hair and makeup again tomorrow just because Kevin couldn't get his shit together. And now everything's going to look unbalanced." She pulled the covers up farther, but her glaring eyes were still visible.

"I can sit out the pictures," Siena said with what Celeste detected was a bit of hope in her voice. Kassie glowered at her.

"What about your dad?" Celeste suggested. "Could he fill in the space?"

Kassie's face looked like she had just suggested that they move the reception down to the bingo hall and serve hot dogs and drink boxes. "No. He's, like, seventy. And his suit is a different color." She looked at Melissa. "Pass me a cinnamon bun."

The door to the room opened and Victoria entered. She paused for a moment and appeared to be steeling herself as though she were preparing for battle. "What are you still doing in bed? The hair-and-makeup team will be here any time for your 'brunch look.'" She looked at Celeste and rolled her eyes. "Don't you want to shower?"

"She's upset about Kevin," said Siena. "And it's 'morning glow,' right, Kassie?"

"Well, we're all upset about Kevin," said Victoria. "But for goodness' sake, it's your wedding day. Get out of bed and enjoy this day your father and I have forked over a fortune for."

Kassie glared at her mother. "Why is it always about you, Mom?"

Victoria's stern gaze frosted over completely, and Celeste winced. She had to intervene. "I have an idea," she said. "You may not like it, but…" The second the words left her mouth she regretted it. It was a ridiculous idea. And would likely be next to impossible to pull off. But Kassie was ridiculous too, so maybe it would fly.

"Well, what is it?" Kassie said.

"Do you remember the guide from yesterday? Who came to pick up the guys for the fishing expedition?"

"Who, the guy with the melt-in-your-mouth chocolate eyes? Um, yeah, he was pretty much unforgettable."

"Well, your fiancé took a real liking to him. And…I think he'd fit into Kevin's suit very nicely. What if—" She paused. "What if he came for the photos so that everything is as you want it for social media?" she said. "And then I can arrange for the photographer to return tomorrow morning to take some really nice family pictures with Kevin in them."

What was she doing? There was no way Jack was going to agree to be part of a wedding-party photo shoot. He clearly hadn't even wanted to touch a rehearsal dinner with a ten-foot pole. But Kassie had a glimmer of interest in her eyes, so she'd worry about that later.

"Oh, for goodness' sake, you and your social media," Victoria scoffed. She looked at Celeste, her lips as tight as her bun was wound. "Have you ever worked with a bride like this?"

Celeste maintained a neutral expression. In the world of weddings, especially with a family like the Harris family, she was Switzerland, although inside she was definitely Team Victoria. "All I want is for Kassie to have the wedding of her dreams." She looked at Kassie, who swung her legs over the side of the bed and stood up.

"Get him," Kassie said, as though having Jack come to their wedding to stand in for Kevin was as easy as booking one of his tours. She snatched her silk robe from the chair beside the bed. "He is a bona fide hunk. He'll look perfect in photos, and I think I prefer him to Kevin anyway. I'm going to shower." With that, she disappeared into the bathroom and slammed the door, leaving Celeste with Victoria and the bridesmaids, who were all giving each other the same look they'd probably given each other many times before this day.

"If you need anything else, please let me know," Celeste said. She exited the room to the quiet of the hallway and stared down at her list.

9 a.m., she scrawled in the margin. *Pray for a miracle.*

She was a master of details, but this was a stretch. Now she had some magic to perform.

JACK GROANED IN relief as he flopped back onto his couch. Bodie leapt up and occupied the spot beside him as he flicked on the television and found a basketball game. He took a sip of his coffee and scratched Bodie's head with his free hand.

He'd gotten up and done a hard workout that morning at the gym and was happy to have a free day with nothing to do but flick between the news and sports and order takeout.

He thought about Celeste, back at the lodge, and how her workday was likely just beginning. The group had been a lot of fun, despite the small matter of the flasks, but he'd seen way worse, and they'd been mostly sober by the time he'd brought them back.

Celeste had been a big part in the success of the day. The river never disappointed, and any time they brought home a decent catch he felt like he'd done his job, but when they'd arrived back for lunch to see the feast that Celeste had put out and how she'd made it look so nice even though they'd been wet and muddy and not at all looking like a group prepared for fine dining, he'd been wowed. It was amazing how that moment had elevated the rest of the day, and Jack could tell the group had been impressed.

And then there was the kiss, electric and exhilarating. A moment that had been on replay since she'd slipped back into the lodge's foyer and he'd sat in his truck for a minute, unable to suppress the grin that had spread across his face. The warmth of her embrace still enveloped him, and he knew the inevitable was happening: He was falling for her.

As if his daydream about her prompted Celeste to think

of him, his phone started to buzz on the couch beside him with her name on the call display, and his heart skipped a beat, anticipation coursing through him like a current.

"Hey," he said. "How's it going over there?"

"We're just about to serve brunch," Celeste's voice came through, her words laced with a hint of something unspoken, stirring something in him. "So, I won't keep you long. But you were a real hit yesterday. The guys had a great time."

"It was a lot of fun," Jack said. "Is anyone in the dog-house?"

"Actually, I think the bride and her bridesmaids might have been more buzzed than the men, to tell you the truth," she said. "So, I apologize for overreacting. Thanks again for all your help. You were amazing."

He appreciated the compliment, but was there something a bit over-the-top about the effusiveness of her words? "No apology needed," Jack said. "And happy to help. Let me know if you need anything else." He'd be more than happy to help Celeste again. And the association with the Butterfly Lake Lodge could be a new source of revenue. They'd already sent an e-transfer with the agreed-upon fee and a nice tip, which he appreciated.

The line was quiet for a moment. "Funny you ask..." Celeste said. "But, uh, ever considered a side hustle in modeling?"

Jack scoffed. "Oh yeah, definitely. I had an agent there for a while, but I was only getting offered contracts for

Calvin Klein underwear ads, and I'm a bit on the shy side."

The line went quiet again. Celeste cleared her throat. "I'm not kidding, actually. The last groomsman's flight was canceled, and he won't make it here until lunch tomorrow, if he's lucky. The bride is—how do I say it?—*particular* about having a balanced bridal party in her wedding photos."

"Uh-huh," Jack said. "Explain to me how I fit into this equation?"

"Come to the wedding?" Celeste said. "Even just the ceremony and pictures? Pose for a few photos and eat some dynamite hors d'oeuvres and be on your way before dinner?"

"You've got to be kidding me. Why would they want a stranger in their wedding photos forever?" While he was eager to see Celeste again, if there was anything he hated almost more than weddings, it was posing for pictures.

"They *liked* you, Jack! And like I said, the bride is…particular."

"And I hate weddings."

"Please?" Celeste said.

"No."

"I'll come fishing."

"Now I know you're desperate."

"I will. I'll experience everything so I can recommend you to more guests."

"You wouldn't already?"

"Hah," said Celeste. "I want to be able to speak with authority."

"Well, unfortunately I don't have a suit." There. If the bride was as particular as Celeste was making her out to be, he figured she wouldn't want him there in his khakis and a sweatshirt.

"What kind of man doesn't have a suit?"

"The kind that likes having an excuse not to attend fancy events."

"Well, lucky for you, Kevin's suit was shipped here, and I think you're around the same size. And I'll make you another batch of that stew."

He felt his defenses chipping away. It was less about the promises she was making and more about the sweet, slightly breathy sound of Celeste's voice and the idea of her needing something from him that was too much for him to fight against. That addictive brush of her lips against his and the promise of maybe more.

"Please, Jack?" she said, and he was done.

"Lucky for me, huh?" Jack said, squeezing his eyes shut and flopping back onto the couch. Where was his willpower? Any iota of good sense? "Fine. What time?"

Chapter Ten

BRUNCH WENT OFF without a hitch, the morning sunlight spilling through the gallery and enhancing Kassie's bronzer-induced glow in a way that Celeste could tell made her very pleased. Guests raved about the mango eggs benny and the frittata, and everyone seemed happy with the choices of activities to keep them busy until the wedding.

Later in the afternoon, Celeste returned to the bridal suite to check on things. In contrast to the morning, hushed voices sounded from behind the suite's door as she approached. She paused for a moment, gauging if it was the right time to knock or if perhaps Jeff had made a visit to the suite to see his bride. Most people kept up with the tradition of not seeing one another until the bride walked down the aisle, but Celeste had been surprised once before by a couple who'd wanted to...*be intimate* on their wedding morning, and she would never make that assumption again.

After listening for a few seconds, it was clear that Jeff wasn't in the room. She lifted her fist to rap on the door just as the door flung open.

Victoria rolled her eyes at Celeste as she breezed by in her robe. "She's in a mood again," she said, leaving Celeste standing in the doorway.

Celeste stepped into the room. "I'm just here to check if anyone needs anything," she said tentatively. "Are you enjoying your wedding day so far?"

Kassie was sitting on the bed, rubbing a jade roller on her forehead. "The water here isn't good for my skin," she said, glaring at Celeste. This was a new one.

"I could have someone bring up a pitcher of filtered water," Celeste said. "From the mountain springs nearby." She had no idea if that would be the difference maker Kassie was looking for, but she said it with confidence anyway.

"It's too late," Kassie said, moving the jade roller to the skin under her eyes. "You should really get some water softeners in here." The softness and vulnerability she had shown the night before had disappeared in a puff of setting powder.

"Well, I think your skin is absolutely glowing," Celeste said. "With no puffiness at all." She gave her a quick smile.

Kassie glanced sideways at her sisters. Melissa was busy steaming her satin gown, and Siena was removing the balled-up tissue paper from her high heels.

Celeste took a seat next to Kassie on the bed. "Are you feeling better than last night?" she said quietly.

Kassie nodded. "All good." It was clear she didn't want to speak any more about it, and that was fine with Celeste.

She stood up. "Glad to hear it. I'll check in again in a

little while. Oh, and Jack will be here around five."

That got a grin from Kassie. "Nice work," she said.

Put that on your socials, Celeste thought as she went to check on things downstairs.

Setup was almost complete in the great room when Celeste arrived. She moved through the space, examining the floral arch by the windows, the cocktail bar, and the buffet table in the conservatory.

Jeff had gone with her recommendation of the floral chandelier, and the great room was now presided over by an astonishing cascade of delicate blooms in shades of blush pink, ivory, and soft lavender, with roses, peonies, and hydrangeas spilling forth from the intricate framework. It was a showstopper.

In a quiet lull, Celeste excused herself to her office. She took a moment to open her email and found a message from Gus Evans. It was a forward of the job posting at the Keystone Ridge Resort. Celeste scanned through the text.

Classification: *Full-time, permanent*

About Us: *The Keystone Ridge Resort is a prestigious destination renowned for unparalleled luxury, exceptional service, and exquisite experiences. Nestled in the heart of Alberta's Rocky Mountains, our hotel embodies elegance, sophistication, and a commitment to providing guests with unforgettable moments of indulgence.*

Job Description: *As the Director of Guest Experience, you will be responsible for overseeing all aspects of operations to ensure the highest standards of excellence are main-*

*tained. This role requires a dynamic leader with a passion
for luxury hospitality, a keen eye for detail, and a proven
track record of success in managing upscale properties.*

So far, so good. She'd only managed a property, singular,
but the Butterfly Lake Lodge would definitely qualify as
luxury.

She continued to scan through the key responsibilities,
which included everything from *Lead and inspire a team of
department heads and staff to deliver exceptional service and
exceed guest expectations* to *Maintain impeccable standards of
cleanliness, maintenance, and safety to uphold the hotel's
reputation for luxury and sophistication.* Okay, she could do
that.

When she got to the qualifications section, two of the
eight requirements made her stomach sink a little.

Qualifications:

- *Bachelor's degree in Hospitality Management, Business
  Administration, or related field; master's degree preferred*
- *Minimum of ten years of experience in luxury hotel
  management, with a proven track record of success in a
  leadership role*

She had no business applying for this job.

Just as she was about to delete the email, her phone
pinged with a message from Gus. "*Just go for it,*" he wrote.
Clearly he saw right through her when she said she was
inquiring for a friend. "*What have you got to lose?*"

She stared at her phone, her mind whirling. *My pride?*

WHAT IN THE hell did you agree to? Jack thought as he sat in his truck outside the Butterfly Lake Lodge. Was it too late to back out?

The last wedding he'd been to had been for his brother and Julie, four years earlier at a reception hall in a suburb just outside of Calgary. He'd been asked to make a speech, which had resulted in at least three sleepless nights and only a smattering of polite applause and had to do everything he could not to roll his eyes when Caden and Julie had had their first dance to a Celine Dion song.

It had been painful. And they were his *family.*

What he was about to walk into might be a whole new sublayer of hell.

The only thing keeping him from doing a three-point turn and beelining it right back to the highway was the promise of continued business from the McCarthys. From what he understood, Celeste's dad usually led the excursions, but they didn't include river expeditions, so he might be able to snag a booking or two a week.

The idea of seeing Celeste again might have factored into things too.

When he entered the lodge's reception area, a woman with short gray hair, a pale blue dress, and a wide smile was passing through with an empty tray. The sounds of a piano floated through from the great room, and the whole space smelled of fresh bread and scented candles.

"You must be Jack," the woman said. She deposited the tray onto the reception desk and extended her hand. "Jeannie McCarthy."

Jack accepted the handshake. Celeste had her mother's eyes—that was for sure. "Beautiful place you have here, Mrs. McCarthy," he said. "And you make one hell of a biscotti."

Jeannie smiled. "The guys haven't stopped talking about the trip yesterday. You really saved us," she said. "On behalf of my husband, who's still up in bed under the weather, and myself, thank you so very much." The woman was as elegant as she was friendly, and he could see how she'd managed to keep customers coming back for so many years.

"It's my pleasure," he said. He didn't like lying through his teeth, but he couldn't very well tell the truth.

"You're also a real sport," she said, taking Jack's coat. She leaned in and lowered the volume of her voice. "Between you and me, I can't believe this is happening."

"Gotta keep your guests happy," he said. "Celeste seems pretty great at that."

"The best," said Jeannie. "Let me take you to one of the rooms to change." She led him down the hallway away from the reception desk, then motioned to an open door that had a number six on it. He assumed it was where the missing brother and groomsman was meant to have stayed. "Here's the suit." She led him to the closet, where a gray suit was hanging along with a white dress shirt and a burgundy tie. "I'll leave you to it," Jeannie said. "Everyone's in the great room when you're ready."

She closed the door behind her. Alone in the room, Jack glanced around at his surroundings. The space was cozy and well decorated, with furniture that Jack could tell was of fine quality. He approached the window to take in the view of Butterfly Lake. The water was calm, reflecting the last of the afternoon light. It was a nice day for a wedding, he had to admit.

He shrugged off his sweater and folded his jeans on the bed, then buttoned up the dress shirt and pulled on the suit pants and jacket. This might have been the most ridiculous thing he'd ever done. He felt a flash of annoyance with himself, letting himself get convinced to do something like this. It was like Christine all over again.

But at the same time, it was different. With Christine, it was always about her. Her career, her whims, her goals. Her happiness, over his, every time.

And with Celeste, it seemed like everything she did was to make things work for other people, to make others happy. It was the whole point of her work. He softened a little, thinking of the expression in her eyes when she'd told him she might've been losing her job.

She might've been making him a sucker again. But here he was, and he'd agreed to play along.

He buttoned the cuffs of the shirt, slid on the blazer, then moved to the bathroom to examine the fit in the mirror. Not bad. Kevin was an inch or two taller and Jack's shoulders were ever-so-slightly broader, but aside from that, the suit fit pretty well. It was quality fabric. If Jack were to buy another suit, he'd like one like this.

Celeste had seemed horrified that he didn't own a suit of his own. Something told him that being with a woman like her meant lots of occasions with a certain dress code. Exactly the type of events he did his best to avoid.

He tied the tie and straightened the collar as a knock sounded at the door.

"Coming," he said, half expecting to find the bride, making sure he had a close enough shave or that his hair was styled appropriately, or maybe Kurt checking to see if he needed a flask of his own. He'd welcome that, actually.

When he swung the door open, he found Celeste, wearing black pants, a black blazer, high heels and holding her clipboard. She looked him up and down, a satisfied expression crossing her pretty features. "It's perfect," she said. "You clean up nicely."

"You look great too," he said. He loved her in a suit. Especially with the heels and her shiny hair begging to be touched.

"Just trying to blend into the background," she said. Like she could ever blend in. "You're invited to stay for dinner, by the way," Celeste said.

The thought of spending more time with her at the reception stirred something within him, despite his initial plans to slip away after the photo shoot. "Will I sit with you?" he asked. He was wearing a suit to be in wedding photos. And now he was thinking of extending the torture by staying for a *wedding dinner*?

"With the family," she said. "But I'll be there. I'm working, remember."

"I'd prefer if you sat with me," Jack said, his gaze locked with hers. "But as long as you're there."

The corners of Celeste's lips turned up and her eyes sparkled. "I'd better get out there," she said, her voice sending a bolt of electricity down his spine. "Here—let me fix your collar."

Jack stood still as Celeste approached. As she tossed the clipboard aside and reached out to smooth his collar and lapel, he couldn't help but inhale deeply, intoxicated by the scent of her shampoo that enveloped him like a tantalizing embrace. He smiled a little to himself, noting the way she bit her lower lip while concentrating. He liked being fussed over by Celeste and willed her not to take her hands off of him. He wanted more. He wanted those same hands all over him.

He'd get up and say a speech at this point, if she asked him to. Escort Grandma onto the dance floor. He'd even do the chicken dance.

She stepped back and nodded her approval. "I'll see you in a few minutes?" He didn't want her to leave. He wanted her to slam the door shut, lock it, and completely mess up his suit.

"Ready for my close-up," he said, grinning. "And that suit is nice, but I can't wait to see you in a pair of waders."

Celeste rolled her eyes, a seductive smile tugging at the corners of her lips as she moved through the doorway, starting to pull the door closed behind her. "The things I do for my job."

Chapter Eleven

A S SOON AS she reached the end of the hallway, Celeste took a deep, calming breath but couldn't wipe the smile off her face, never mind ignore the body buzz summoned from being in Jack's sphere, feeling the warmth of the skin on his neck as she'd adjusted the silky-smooth fabric of his collar, his eyes daring her to edge closer. She'd almost succumbed to the temptation and allowed herself to sink back into his arms, let his lips intertwine with hers. Her discipline deserved an award.

She retreated to the office, where she gave herself five minutes to regroup, fix her hair, and pep talk herself into making this wedding a social media sensation.

Focus, she willed herself. Every moment for the next eight or more hours demanded that she be at her best.

When she entered the great room, the officiant had just arrived and was organizing her paperwork at a table near the window, and the bottles of Veuve Clicquot were perfectly chilled and ready to tip into the waiting crystal flutes for the toast immediately following the ceremony. The jazz trio, a Keystone Ridge staple who were still playing weddings well into their eighties, were adding light background music as Kurt and the newest groomsman mingled with the other guests, awaiting the arrival of the bridesmaids, mother-of-the-bride, and the bride herself.

The nice thing about a small wedding was if they started a few minutes late or early, no one would mind. It felt relaxed and easy, unlike trying to ignore the force of attraction Jack was radiating from where he stood over by the fireplace. Celeste decided she'd better check on things upstairs to make sure there wasn't any last-minute drama to attend to.

The door to what would be the newlyweds' suite tonight was open, and Celeste approached slowly, listening for any bickering or harsh words or, worse, a full-on meltdown. But what she came across was a very tender moment between the bride and her mother as Victoria fastened a necklace around her daughter's neck and then stood back, beaming with pride as Kassie fingered the delicate stone. "Thanks, Mom," she murmured. "I love you."

They embraced, and Celeste swallowed the small lump that had formed from witnessing something so lovely and pure. No matter how many weddings they hosted and how much bickering, drama, and disagreement that came up, there was always a moment that reminded Celeste why she loved days like this.

Kassie looked stunning. She wore a halter-style ivory silk gown with a delicate transparent crystal overlay that hung from her shoulders all the way down to where the fabric lightly grazed the floor and twinkled in the light like she was wearing little stars from head to toe. Her dark hair was pulled back into a tight bun, allowing her pretty features, which the makeup artist had highlighted expertly with the "evening" look, to be the main event. The diamond necklace that she'd just been gifted pulled the look together perfectly.

"You look absolutely gorgeous," Celeste said when it seemed appropriate to enter the room. She looked around at the bridesmaids and the mother of the bride, who also looked like they'd stepped out of the pages of a high-end bridal magazine. "What a beautiful necklace."

Kassie adjusted the stone around her neck. "It was my mother's," said Victoria. "She gave it to me on my wedding day."

Celeste braced herself for Kassie to make a comment about how that marriage had ended up, but instead she hugged her mother again.

"It's perfect," Celeste said. "You all look perfect. What a beautiful family."

The bridesmaids wore pale green dresses in three different styles but all made with the same fabric, which glowed in an iridescent shimmery gold. Victoria was a picture of elegance in a long navy gown, accented with gold jewelry and a sizable emerald ring on her right hand.

Celeste nodded to the clock on the bedside table. "We're about ten minutes out, if you think you're ready," she said.

"I wanted to see if there's anything else you need."

"Just a selfie with you," said Kassie. "You've been amazing!"

Celeste grinned. "Of course," she said, joining the group as Kassie angled her phone and caught them all in the camera's frame, the photographer quietly snapping photos in the background while stepping over the various clothing items, shoe boxes, and shopping bags that littered the room. Celeste made a mental note to return to the room during the reception and tidy up so that the newlyweds didn't return to a complete disaster.

"Victoria, once we see you at the bottom of the stairs, Kurt will come and escort you to your seat. You'll hear the beginning of Pachelbel's Canon, then you two"—she nodded at Melissa and Siena—"will have your escorts as well. Kassie, your father will be ready for you at the bottom of the stairs. Good luck!"

Celeste left the women with the photographer to take some shots of them receiving their bouquets and rejoined the rest of the group in the great room.

All the men looked handsome in their suits, but when Celeste found Jack, perched on the arm of the large camel leather couch, the soft light from the fireplace flickering in his dark eyes, she took a sharp breath in. He was irresistible.

A clean shave accentuated the sharp line of his jaw, and his thick wavy hair was pulled away from his face and tucked behind his ears.

Despite her best efforts, she indulged in some revisionist history that had her kicking the door to his suite closed when she'd been fixing his suit, standing so close she'd been breathing in the pulse-quickening scent of his aftershave, reveling in the feeling of his gaze on her.

If she'd tipped her chin up ever-so-slightly, she knew he would have kissed her again.

The bride was about to make her appearance, but Celeste was having a hard time focusing on much else than what it would feel like to be alone with Jack again. Try as she might to dismiss his outdoorsy inclinations, there was something primal and strong about them at the same time. The fact that he could rock a suit like this was too distracting.

Focus. She stared so hard at her clipboard she was surprised she wasn't boring holes through it. When she glanced up again, Jack was looking right at her, a sexy half smile dancing on his lips, his gaze dripping with desire, like he knew exactly what was playing out in her daydream and was picking right up where she'd left off to let the rest of it unfold in his mind.

She returned his smile, then tore her eyes away from his perfect face. She steeled herself. "Ladies and gentlemen, I'll invite you to take your seats," Celeste said to the group as the groomsmen and father of the bride moved to the back of the room and the jazz trio shuffled their sheet music for the traditional wedding procession.

Jeff stood by the window with the officiant, fiddling with

his cuff links as he shifted from one leg to the other.

Celeste glanced toward the back of the room at Jack, who was chatting good-naturedly with Kurt. Apparently whatever he was saying was very funny. For someone who allegedly hated weddings, it didn't seem like he was having such a terrible time.

When Melissa gave Celeste the signal from the top of the staircase, she nodded to the jazz trio. It was showtime.

The band started to play, and after Victoria took her seat, Melissa and Siena were escorted to their places by Kurt and Jack.

It seemed like every guest in the room had their phones out, capturing images of the bridal party and then the smiling bride as she took her father's elbow, her eyes misty as he kissed her on the cheek. Kassie would have lots of photos to choose from.

Celeste and Jeannie moved to the space near the staircase as soon as the wedding processional had cleared the hallway. They wanted to be on hand if anything was required of them but far enough in the background that they weren't intruding on the intimacy of the event.

The vows were repeated, a kiss was cheered, and after twenty minutes, Celeste was passing out flutes of champagne to a very happy bride and groom and their guests.

When Celeste approached Jack with the tray of drinks, he accepted a glass, then held it up in the air, tipping it toward her. "Cheers to you," he said, the depth of his voice unleashing a cascade of shivers over her skin. "Seems like everything's going off without a hitch."

"Don't jinx it," she said, smiling. "We still have the whole reception for something to go wrong."

"Excuse me, you two," Jeannie said. She placed her hand on Jack's elbow. "I don't mean to interrupt, but are you ready for your close-up, Jack?"

Jack passed Celeste his flute and straightened his collar. He looked at her. "What do you think? Am I ready?"

You're perfect, she thought, but she could only nod. Celeste watched as Jack joined the rest of the bridal party by the fireplace, the reluctant but appreciated and completely disarming interloper.

WHILE THE PHOTOGRAPHER directed the group, Celeste took the opportunity to go back to the kitchen to sit for a few minutes and give her throbbing feet a rest. She found Quinn at the table, with a cup of tea and a scone beside her as she worked on a sudoku puzzle.

"How's it going out there?" said Quinn.

"We'll have some good shots for you to post," Celeste said. Wedding pictures were always popular, and Quinn was skilled in using hashtags to gain new followers. She poured herself a glass of water from the dispenser and joined her sister. "Just make sure you get the couple's approval on everything first. And the photographer's."

"Of course. How's Jack?"

"He's fine, I think," Celeste said. "I've agreed to have dinner with him tonight." A totally stupid and irrational decision, but she couldn't very well go back on it now that the bride and groom had arranged for a place for her at a table.

Quinn looked up, eyes wide. "Wait, you're his date?"

"No, I think he just felt kind of obligated to stay for dinner. And he doesn't really know anyone, plus there's the extra place setting for Kevin and his girlfriend." It sounded less ridiculous when she said it out loud.

"Well, you can't wear that," Quinn said, eyeing her suit.

"Why not? I've been wearing it all day."

"Exactly. Go get changed," her sister urged. "I'll go check to see if anything is needed out there. And definitely go with that silver dress you bought from Revolve."

Celeste considered. Her suit was very appropriate for work. But she had been wearing it since six a.m., and Kassie would probably prefer her in something a bit more formal if she happened to get in the background of any photos. "Fine. All right, thanks. I won't be long."

"Toodel-oo," said Quinn, turning back to her puzzle.

Celeste left through the door off the kitchen, where the catering staff was unloading the last trays of hors d'oeuvres. Jeannie and Mariana were making some of the key parts of the meal, but a group this size required outside support.

The sun was just starting to set behind the tree line across the lake as she crossed the parking lot between the lodge and her cabin. Breathing in the cool, clean air had a steadying effect.

"Hope you're not standing me up," she heard from behind her. She turned to find Jack standing to the side of the building, car keys in hand.

"I'm just going to get changed," Celeste said. "You look like you're ready to escape. Are the photos already done?"

"They're doing family photos now. Apparently I'm due back in five minutes." He motioned to his truck. "Just grabbing my overnight bag," he said. "If I'm going to have a couple drinks, I'll take your mom up on the offer of staying in Kevin's room. That bed looks like a dream."

The idea of Jack staying overnight at the lodge ignited a rush of anticipation. Which was silly. They wouldn't even be under the same roof. But the idea of him lingering for more than just a few hours, the possibility of stealing some moments alone together was exciting. But that couldn't happen. She was his date, technically, but still needed to behave like the manager of this event that she was.

Time to change the subject from beds or sleeping or anything resembling being in a bed and not sleeping. She cleared her throat. "My mom is very appreciative of everything you've done over the past couple of days. Don't be surprised if you start getting more calls in the coming weeks. We've got a pretty packed house. For the time being, at least."

"You mean until they sell?"

"Yup," said Celeste. She'd managed to forget about it for most of the day and now unease was creeping up again. But it wasn't the time to dwell on the future. "Anyway, I'm going to get changed."

"Not sure why. You look great to me," Jack said, that same irresistible grin playing on his lips.

Celeste felt a flutter in her chest but quickly pushed it aside. "Thank you," she said. "But I've been wearing this all day. And everyone else is so dressed up. I'll see you in a few minutes." She made toward her cabin again.

"Celeste," Jack called.

She turned back.

His gaze held a magnetic intensity that sent a rush of heat creeping up her neck. "I meant what I said—you're doing an amazing job." With a wave and a lingering look, he closed the door of his truck and returned to the lodge, leaving Celeste just a little bit breathless and fully exhilarated.

It was nice to have someone validate her work. Her parents were always complimentary, but she often chalked that up to the fact that they seemed to think anything that their four daughters did was worthy of praise.

Hearing it from Jack, though, as someone who seemed to roll his eyes at weddings, felt really good.

In her room, Celeste changed into the silver dress Quinn had suggested. She added a pair of hoop earrings and slipped on a dressier pair of heels and reapplied her lipstick. She had a date. Sure, she was technically still working, but Jack was there because of her. And she wanted to look good for him.

She poured herself half a glass of white wine from her fridge and took a moment to sit at her breakfast bar and have a quiet moment to herself before rejoining the party. She always liked to take a minute or two during a busy event to sit and think. What was going well? What still needed doing? What undercurrents was she picking up on, and how could she get ahead of them?

The rollout of events was going perfectly. No need to worry about the food or drinks; Jeannie and Mariana had that under control, and Quinn and the caterers would be helping.

The one thing she might need to do was to find a subtle way to suggest to Kassie to express her thanks to her parents, not just in a speech but toward the end of the night. She heard it all the time from brides and grooms that the day flew by so quickly that they barely had a chance to think, and while there were some people who Celeste could tell would be able to think about others in addition to themselves on this kind of day, Kassie wasn't one of them, and she knew how much it would mean to Victoria and Gary.

They were footing the bill, a substantial one, and while all parents just wanted to see their children happy, everyone liked feeling appreciated.

Aside from that, she made a mental note to ensure the

bridal party's water pitchers were topped up at their tables and not to forget the engraved sterling-silver cake server that the lodge always gave as a gift to the married couple to cut their cake.

She also had to keep her head on straight around Jack. He was altogether too handsome, and after the wedding, Celeste needed to turn all of her attention back to her accounting course and her job search. This silly crush couldn't get in the way of that.

She checked her appearance once more in the mirror, fussed with her hair a bit, then went to join the reception.

The twenty-four guests were enjoying cocktails and passed hors d'oeuvres in the great room, which was glowing with the rich orangey light from the setting sun over the lake, casting the shadow of the mountain peaks.

You look great! mouthed Quinn from across the room, where she was replenishing the napkins. Celeste straightened her shoulders. She felt good. And being a guest at the Butterfly Lake Lodge instead of an employee was kind of nice too.

It didn't take long for her to spot Jack standing by the fire again with what looked like a scotch on ice, conversing with the father of the bride. Celeste plucked a drink from one of the waiters' trays—the themed cocktail of the evening, which was called Orchard Catch, a nod to the place where Kassie and Jeff had met while berry-and-apple picking. It was made with fresh strawberries and elderflower liqueur topped with sparkling wine. She took a sip, and as Jack caught her eye from across the room, he gave her a slight smile that unleashed a kaleidoscope of butterflies in her stomach.

She was about to cross the room to join him when Kurt appeared beside her. "Cheers," he said, holding up his wineglass and giving her a wide grin. "You guys did a bang-up job with this wedding."

Celeste forced a smile. "Thanks," she said. "Much appreciated." When she glanced back at Jack, he was watching her with that sexy lopsided grin. *Save me*, she willed him. But he knew just as well as she did that it wasn't his place at this party. She was a host, and she could take care of herself.

"So, you worked here for a long time?" Kurt said.

How original, Celeste thought.

Kurt launched into an introduction to himself and his life. He was a journalist for an online entertainment publication who'd gone to university with Jeff. He played pickleball and was into vintage cars.

"I'll have to introduce you to my sister Quinn," Celeste said, noting a flash of disappointment in Kurt's expression. He was handsome, and aside from being a tad self-centered, he ended up being a decent conversationalist, and any other time Celeste might have been okay to spend the evening talking with someone like him, but tonight she felt Jack's presence like a firm pull, and it was a real effort to focus on Kurt and his questions.

She kept Jack in the corner of her eye as a couple of the other guests joined his conversation. He was telling a story, and the small group around him were all ears.

When it felt like an appropriate break, Celeste excused herself from Kurt. "I'm going to check on the kitchen," she said, even though Jeannie had taken over and urged her to have a nice evening. "If you haven't tried the feature cocktail, you should give it a try. It's amazing." Before Kurt could respond, she smiled and made her exit, congratulating herself on how smooth it was. No one would call Celeste McCarthy rude.

When she walked by where Jack was still holding court, she gave him a quick wave, and he responded with a lift of his glass and that familiar, irresistible tilt of his lips that always seemed meant just for her. With a surge of warmth blooming in her chest, Celeste continued to the kitchen, where her mother was overseeing the catering staff. Jeannie stood in the doorway, blocking her entry. "How's it going in here, Mom?"

"Good. And you don't need to worry about a thing. I don't know about these Yorkshire puddings," Jeannie said under her breath. "But look at you!" She stepped back and looked Celeste up and down. "Honey, you look gorgeous!" She raised an eyebrow. "I'm sure that Jack has noticed too."

"Would everyone leave me alone about Jack?" Celeste said.

"Go back to the party. Everything's under control in

here."

It took everything in her, but Celeste did her best to keep things on simmer during the dinner, even between the second course and dessert, when she looked across the table to find Jack's eyes undressing her unabashedly. She pulled from a deep well of restraint to pretend not to notice and instead make small talk with Uncle Jasper, who was seated next to her.

Jack didn't give up easily, though. After dessert, when he moved his leg against hers under the table, the feeling of his silky suit brushing up against her bare skin was more than she could take, and she'd had to excuse herself to the washroom to cool off, her pulse thrumming as she tried to maintain her composure.

THE REST OF the wedding unrolled with the characteristic clockwork perfection that the Butterfly Lake Lodge was renowned for. Shortly after eleven, after sparklers and a final dance, the bride and groom bid farewell to their guests to return to their suite. Celeste, Quinn, and Jeannie did a sweep of the great room to extinguish candles, pick up any remaining glassware, and offer one last round of refreshments to any guests who were still awake.

Of course, the guests were free to stay up as long as they wished, but Jeannie was more than ready for bed, and

Celeste wouldn't be far behind.

When she went to check on the puzzle room, she found Jack sitting in a leather chair, flipping through the pages of the Agatha Christie novel he'd pulled out the other day. He'd taken off his tie at a certain point and the top couple of buttons of his shirt were undone, and impossibly, he looked even more handsome than before.

He looked up when she entered, his eyes lighting with warmth. "My hands are clean," he said. "I promise to return it in perfect condition." He held up his hands as proof.

"We're not too precious about it," said Celeste. "Books are meant to be read."

Jack's lips turned up slightly. "Great work today," he said. "You might have me changing my mind about weddings."

She smiled back, keeping to the edge of the entrance as though getting too close to Jack would allow the superpowered magnet of attraction between them to remove any and all of her willpower. "I'm glad you had a good time."

"Something tells me you're going to have no problem at all finding a job if it doesn't work out here," he said, then tried to cover up a yawn. "The bed in that room looks pretty inviting right about now." He stood up and placed the book back on the shelf.

"Get some sleep," Celeste said. "And get ready for breakfast in the morning."

"I'll be up and out of here before you wake up, probably," Jack said. "I've got to get home to walk Bodie."

It was probably for the best that he was disappearing at the crack of dawn, as though he'd never been there, but a pang of disappointment hit her.

Celeste walked with Jack to his room. The hallway was empty, and the only sound was the din from the great room, where someone had gotten a game of gin rummy going. "Well, good night," she said.

In the dim light of the hallway, Jack turned to face her. "'Night, Celeste," he said.

She sensed hesitation in his voice. Was he waiting for her to do something?

"Good night, Jack," she said again and made a move back toward the office.

Before she could leave, she felt his fingers interlock with hers, his hand tugging her toward him softly. She looked up to see his eyes burning with desire.

"I shouldn't—" She stopped, her protest dying on her lips as she met his smoldering gaze. She took shallow breaths in, but she couldn't move away.

"You don't have to explain yourself," Jack said, the low timbre of his voice making her quake. He moved his face closer to hers and spoke quietly into her ear. "I just needed to tell you how beautiful you looked tonight. And how impressive you are. That's all." He pulled away slightly and kissed her hand, and it was so smooth and gentlemanly she thought she might explode. She was melting into a puddle on the floor. "Good night, Celeste."

"Wait," she whispered. She drew in a sharp breath as her mouth parted slightly and felt his hand move to the nape of her neck, drawing her in closely as he kissed her softly. She closed her eyes, every gentle sweep of Jack's lips awakening every nerve ending in a delicious thrill.

When the sound of chanting came from the great room, Celeste pulled back. "I'd better go see what's going on," she whispered between shallow breaths.

Jack's eyes flickered with desire. "I can come—"

"It's okay," she said. "You get some sleep." She needed him. Badly. But she also needed to think this through. "I'll see you Monday, right?"

Jack swallowed, then nodded. "You bet. G' night, Celeste."

After his door clicked shut, she leaned up against the wall for a moment, closed her eyes, and took a deep breath in.

Monday was two days away. She'd finish this wedding, then take some time to think things through before falling into what felt like it could actually be something real.

Chapter Twelve

T HE MORNING FOG had just about lifted, and the sun was starting to burn through the light hazy cloud cover overhead. The air was still, and the only sound down at the river was the gentle current rippling through the river rocks and the occasional burbling call of an American dipper, one of the only birds that stuck the course through the winter in the area.

It was the Monday after the wedding, and Jack had been sitting on a fallen-over log, waiting for the past twenty minutes for the rumble of Celeste's Jeep down the path. In the meantime, he was enjoying the stillness and the warm coffee in his thermos.

When Celeste finally pulled into the small gravel lane toward the Bow River access, he stood up and went to greet her.

She rolled down the window and pulled off her sunglasses. "I'm okay to park here?" she asked. She was wearing a thick gray wool sweater and faded blue jeans, a light blue knit hat over her dark hair, which was loose around her shoulders. She was also wearing makeup, he noted, an unusual choice for a day on the river. But he wasn't complaining. She looked dynamite.

"Yeah, just pull in over by my truck," he said, then stood back as she did.

Celeste stepped out of her car and surveyed the area, then looked at Jack, an amused but slightly weary expression on her face. "Okay, teach," she said, pulling an envelope from her pocket and holding it up. "Which one of my creations are we putting to work today?"

Jack chuckled. "Those are for you to keep. I brought a few that we won't mind losing." He indicated to the pile of gear he'd set up by the river. "We need to get you outfitted first."

"Hold on," Celeste said. She moved to the passenger side of her Jeep, where she deposited her envelope of flies made in class, and removed a small blue cooler, then joined him on the path.

"What's that?" Jack said.

"In case we get hungry." She opened the cooler to reveal an entire picnic tucked inside. "Turkey-and-sweet-onion-relish sandwiches, kale-and-Parmesan salad, and fresh-baked oatmeal cookies. Just in case."

"You must be gunning for an A+," he said, grinning. "Or trying to distract me from what we're here to do."

"Always," said Celeste. "And never. All right, what do I do?"

Jack passed Celeste a pair of navy-blue waders that

looked about her size. "Put these on," he said. He smiled to himself as she inspected the waders, then struggled to keep her balance as she slid into the legs of the pants. He held out an arm, which she grasped on to.

"Thanks," she said and stood up. "How do I look?"

She looked like someone he wanted to scoop up into his arms, carry over to the back of his truck, lay out a blanket, and spend a day under the sun with. Not many people could make fly-fishing waders look sexy. And yet there was Celeste, her green eyes sparkling and her hair cascading down the back of the suspenders like she was about to walk down a runway. "Like you stepped right out of the latest issue of *American Angler*," Jack said.

She raised an eyebrow. "I'll pretend you just said *Vogue*."

He inspected the fit. "May I?" he asked, indicating to the straps, which hung a bit loose and would likely slip off her shoulders. Celeste nodded, and he adjusted the length so that they fit snugly. "Here," he said and clicked the waist fastener together, doing his best to avoid brushing his hands against her chest, even though there were many layers of fabric in between them. His mind flashed to the incredible silvery dress that had draped so perfectly over her body the other night, in a way that had made it impossible to prevent his gaze from grazing over her gorgeous figure several times over the course of the evening.

Celeste smiled, and the light of her expression made Jack's stomach do a tumbling routine. "All right, let's do this," she said. "Wait." She stuck her hand down the side of her waders, feeling around for something in her pocket. She pulled out her phone and passed it to him. "Can you take a photo of me? My dad won't believe it unless he sees it."

"Of course," said Jack. He passed Celeste a fishing rod. "Here, hold this. Gotta look the part."

He laughed to himself as he took a picture of her, holding the fishing rod so awkwardly and incorrectly. "Hold on a sec," he said. He took her right hand and placed it on the handle, then angled the rod so that she wouldn't poke her own eye out with the hook. "There. That's better." He paused for a moment before stepping back, a thick magnetic current almost begging him to stay as close as possible to Celeste. She cocked her head to the side, the delight in her eyes keeping him under her spell.

"Do I look authentic now?" she asked.

"Perfect," he said. He meant it in every sense of the word.

The conditions were ideal for a beginner, and Jack had purposely chosen this part of the riverbed for the shallowness as well as the lightness of the current.

"It's actually really pretty out here," she said, following him into the river.

"You sound surprised," said Jack. "Maybe you're more outdoorsy than you thought."

"I'm not *not* outdoorsy," said Celeste. "I'm just more of a…domicile devotee."

Jack couldn't help the laugh that escaped. "I like that. Okay, time to get you in touch with your inner 'alfresco aficionado.'"

It was Celeste's turn to laugh, and the way her eyes lit up made him fall for her even more in that moment.

He spent a few minutes showing her the basics and then letting her try a few casts on her own. It didn't take long before Celeste had a tug on her line.

"You got one. Steady, steady now." He helped her pull the line in, then cupped the small trout in his hands and held it out for her to inspect. It flopped in his hands a little.

"Poor thing," said Celeste, frowning. She looked down at the trout. "I apologize. Let's get you back out there."

Jack gently dislodged the hook from the trout's cheek. When he looked up, she was wincing. "He'll be all right," he said.

"I'm not sure I believe you that that doesn't hurt them," she said.

"Well, they've never told me otherwise." He put the fish back into the water, and they watched as it disappeared in the current. "Want to try for another?"

"I'm good!" said Celeste. "Let's just end on a high note."

Jack chuckled. They'd been out on the river for less than twenty minutes. "Well, I didn't expect to make a convert out of you."

He motioned for her to go first toward the riverbed, then waded behind her. They approached some fallen logs that would do well for a seat and almost collided when Celeste stopped abruptly and turned to face him.

"You're not just a good teacher in the classroom," she said. "I think things are going to pick up for you soon," she said.

He was about to answer when the obnoxious and unmistakable sound of a Hummer engine growled to a halt over where they'd parked. Jack looked over to find Forrest pulling right up next to his truck. He'd gotten his vehicle wrapped with his company logo, with a matching trailer for his gear. "Not if this guy has anything to do with it."

"Who's that?"

"You haven't heard of Forrest Halpern?" Jack said. "I guess you're not spending enough time with the riffraff around here."

"Is he a *Halpern* Halpern?" Celeste said.

"Yup," said Jack. "Not sure he inherited any of his family's brains, though."

They watched as Forrest hopped out of the Hummer, a wide smile on his face. It looked like he was growing out the scruff on his face, but it didn't help him look any older. "Beauty day!" he called, then approached where they were standing.

"Forrest," said Jack. *Screw off*, he wanted to add.

Forrest extended his hand to Celeste. "I don't think I've seen you around town," he said. "I would have remembered. I'm Forrest."

Jack fought back the urge to clock the cocky SOB.

"Celeste," she said and shook his hand. "You run tours out of this area too?"

"I'm starting to," Forrest said. "Are you looking for a guide?"

Jack gritted his teeth as he zeroed in on the perfect spot to land a sharp uppercut to Forrest's jaw.

"I'm all set," Celeste said, placing her hand on Jack's arm. The gesture cooled him just enough to keep him from doing something stupid.

Forrest looked at Jack and raised an eyebrow. "Private lessons, eh, Wallace? I'll have to give that a go." He looked back at Celeste and dug a business card out of his vest. "I'll pass this along, just in case. Or if you have any friends."

Celeste looked sideways at Jack, a slight grin on her face that told him she was just humoring Forrest. "Thank you," she said. She looked over at the Hummer. "That's a whole lot of truck."

"You know what they say," Jack said. "Big truck—"

Forrest laughed. "You're funny, man. Are you done out here? I've got a group coming by in a half an hour. We can share the space. Just let me know where you're going to be. I'll have to set up for photos."

"You know, it's bad form to intrude on a space someone else is using."

"It's public land. We both have licenses, right?"

Jack's blood boiled. But he didn't want to lose it in front

of Celeste. He cared a lot what she thought about him. She was a consummate pro, and he was digging deep to stay calm. "We're about done here," he managed, through gritted teeth. "But this section of the river is where I take my groups. So, feel free to do your thing here today, but it's good etiquette to stake your claim in your own spot." He had to congratulate himself for how evenly that came out.

"All right," said Forrest. "Thanks, Wallace." Jack nodded to Celeste. Maybe they could move someplace else, even though he hated ceding his territory. "But, uh, Wallace," Forrest continued. "I mean, you're really only taking groups out, like, what, once a week now? Surely this prime spot shouldn't go unused just because you don't have bookings?"

Professionalism was no longer an option. Jack was going to kill this twerp.

"Jack's going to have plenty of groups out here now that he's working with my family's business," Celeste said.

Forrest raised an eyebrow. "Your family business? What's that?"

"The Butterfly Lake Lodge," she said, a hint of challenge in her voice.

"Nice place," Forrest said. "A little old-timey, but some of my clients are into that. Happy to recommend it to them, if you want to pass my name along in return."

Through his rage, Jack had to hand it to the kid. He knew how to network.

"Thanks," Celeste said. "We're pretty booked up for the

time being, but that's kind of you." She reached out again and grabbed on to Jack's bicep. "Let's go," she said. "I want to hear more about your time working in Argentina. It sounds incredible."

It was obvious she was going over the top and that she wanted to pump him up in front of Forrest. But he was lapping up every second of it, especially when he noted the jealous glint in Forrest's expression.

"See you around," Jack said as they moved onto shore.

"Forrest Outfitters!" Forrest called from the river. "Don't forget the name!"

Celeste took a hold of Jack's arm as they walked toward the car. "That was some restraint you showed there, teach," she said.

"You could tell?"

"There's still smoke coming from your ears." She fished the keys from her pocket. "I wasn't kidding—I want to know more about your trips. Follow me to the lodge? We can sit out on the dock. I don't want this lunch to go to waste."

Jack swallowed, taking in Celeste's playful expression and the way the sun had already made the light freckles on her nose come out. "Sure thing," he said. All the annoyance and anger he'd felt from talking to Forrest had disappeared. He'd follow her anywhere.

THE AFTERNOON SUN was warm, and a gentle breeze came off the water as they settled into the chairs at the edge of the lodge's dock.

"Last class tonight," Celeste said. "Think you'll do it again?"

Jack considered. Now that he'd done it once, it would be a lot easier the second time around. And he was enjoying it more than he'd expected. "It won't be as much fun without you there," he said.

He watched as Celeste unpacked the picnic basket, and accepted the sandwich rolled up in brown butcher paper and the salad in a glass container. "Here," she said and gave him cutlery rolled up in a cloth napkin.

She noticed him smiling at the striped napkin. "I don't know why you think it's so amusing," she said.

"It's not. I like it," he said, then paused. "And I like you."

Celeste was quiet. "So, you're unattached?" she said.

"Yep," said Jack. "Just me and Bodie these days."

"And what was before 'these days'?"

He considered. Did he really want to ruin the moment by talking about his ex? He glanced over at Celeste as she took a bite of her sandwich. She actually looked interested.

"My last girlfriend broke things off a couple years ago. I guess I wasn't exciting enough for her."

"What does that mean?" said Celeste.

"She said living here was too quiet, and I guess by extension I was boring too. But something tells me she was just thirsty for more drama in her life. She was always trying to pick fights. It wasn't my thing."

"Doesn't seem like you were too broken up about her leaving," Celeste said.

Jack chuckled to himself. Oh, he'd been broken up, a sad puppy dog. It was a version of himself he never wanted to meet again. "Let's just say I learned something from the experience." He took a bite of his sandwich, and as expected, it was perfect. Or maybe it was just the company and the setting. "This is incredible," he said and wiped the corner of his mouth with a napkin. "And how about you? I find it hard to believe you're single."

"What do you mean, hard to believe? I'm a soon-to-be-unemployed thirty-something who basically lives with her parents."

Jack gave her a look. "Okay, Ms. Dramatic. You know just as well as I do that you're a ten. Smart, gorgeous, thoughtful, and fun."

At his words, her expression shifted. "I haven't really had time to date. My hours don't really lend themselves to social time. So, after Matt and I broke up…"

"When was that?"

"Last summer. And I guess the correct expression is 'after Matt left me.'"

"Complete idiot," Jack said. "Certifiable."

Celeste rolled her eyes, but a smile crossed her face.

"What do you do when you're not teaching?"

"Changing the subject?"

"There's nothing else to say."

"All right," Jack said. "Well, I take Bodie on a couple of long walks each day. There's always stuff to do around the house. I FaceTime with my brother and his wife and my niece." He paused. "Now that I say it out loud, it's no wonder Christine left me."

Celeste grinned. "We're just a couple of left-behinds, aren't we?"

"Seems like it," said Jack. A soft breeze came off the lake, blowing some strands of Celeste's hair onto her face. He watched as she brushed them away, the sight of her pink nails making him smile.

"So, you walk, hang with your family," she said.

"And I go out to my cabin now and then." His cabin, a small structure his grandfather had built years ago, was on one of a very few privately owned small plots of land in the provincial park, and while Jack didn't get out there too often, a flash of being there with Celeste entered his mind. The fire crackling, a great bottle of wine. No TV or internet, so plenty of time for other distractions.

"Where's that? And what do you do there?"

"You know that blue painted rock at the turnoff to where I took the bachelor party?"

"Yeah," said Celeste.

"That's the beginning of the trail that leads to the cabin.

It's about a two-and-a-half-mile hike in."

"What's there to do there that you can't do at your place?" she said.

Jack grinned. Being at the cabin with Celeste would be fun. Getting her there, however, might not be considered as enjoyable in her books. "It's just nice to be somewhere different now and then. Change of scenery."

"I can see that," she said. She was quiet for a few moments. "I've been thinking lately that maybe the sale of the lodge is what I needed to move on. Maybe I've gotten too comfortable here. I could use a change of scenery of my own."

Another breeze rippled across the water, then the turquoise surface smoothed again, so clear you could see right to the lake's bottom. Jack stole a glance at Celeste, whose bright green eyes held a warmth that delivered a jolt of desire. She was lying outstretched on the dock, propped up by her elbows. "I can see why you wouldn't want to leave here, though," he said. "It's spectacular."

"It truly is," she replied softly. "Thanks for today. It was pretty great."

"Glad you liked it," said Jack. "See you down there again tomorrow?"

"I said *pretty* great," Celeste said. "I can think of other ways I'd prefer to spend my time."

"Oh, so can I."

Celeste shot him a look, but she was still smiling. "Plus

won't I see you at class tonight?" She looked at her watch. "I'd better get inside, actually. I have a bunch of stuff to do beforehand."

They packed up the basket, and Celeste walked Jack to his truck.

He'd see her again in a matter of hours, but somehow it wasn't soon enough.

AFTER DOING SPOT checks on three of the rooms, Celeste went back to the office to review the upcoming check-ins for the afternoon. The third-floor turret was reserved for three nights by a single traveler who'd requested a late check-in. She'd upgrade him to a walk-out on the main floor. Another one of the main-floor suites would be occupied for two nights by a couple arriving from Boston, who had noted in their reservation details that they were celebrating a sixtieth birthday and had requested that Celeste make a full suite of dining reservations for them at a place in town and then the next night at the 1888 Chop House at the Banff Springs Hotel. She would make sure a bottle of prosecco and some chocolate-covered strawberries were awaiting them in the room.

And the last booking, a four-night stay for a group of three friends traveling together, was for the two adjoining rooms on the second floor with a partial water view and deep soaker tubs in each room. They'd noted in their reservations that one of the party had a serious nut allergy and also inquired about spa treatments in the area.

Celeste loved catering to each guest's individual requests and always did her best to add an unexpected touch wherever possible. She would make sure that the breakfast buffet had a section that was clearly labeled nut-free and made a mental note to remind Jeannie to prepare those items separately from the rest of the pastries. They had a massage provider who would do on-site appointments. She usually reserved the stargazing room for this, since it wasn't in use during the day.

When she checked her phone, she saw that there was a voicemail waiting for her.

"This is a message for Celeste McCarthy," a reserved male voice sounded. "This is Stephan Jolliet from the Keystone Ridge Resort. We received your application, and we'd like to invite you for an interview on Thursday morning at nine a.m." He continued with details about the location of the interview, but Celeste's mind was whirling, and she had to save the message and replay it to note everything down.

When was the last time she'd interviewed for a job? When she'd applied to A Novel Idea, the independent bookstore in town, for a part-time job in twelfth grade?

She certainly hadn't applied for her job at the lodge. What had started out as a last-minute replacement for Mrs.

Hammond, who'd taken on operating the front desk five years after the lodge had opened and the administrative tasks had become too much for Jeannie and Everett. Mrs. Hammond's twenty-one-year-old son and his girlfriend had found themselves in quite a predicament after they'd accidentally gotten pregnant—with twins, and Mrs. Hammond had moved to Surrey to be closer and to help them out.

Celeste had never seen herself working at the lodge. Her plan had been to travel with her friend Emily through Greece and Italy, and she had agreed to help out before and after in order to fund part of the trip, but when they'd found themselves without Mrs. Hammond right at their busiest time of year, Celeste had postponed her trip until her parents found a replacement.

The summer job, which had also helped pay her last year's tuition at the University of Victoria, had extended into a full-time gig after graduation while she'd finished her applications to grad school. She'd been accepted to two different programs but had declined both offers, since Matt had wanted to stay in town, and she'd made the mistake of putting his wants and needs first. Luckily she enjoyed working at the lodge and figured she'd enroll in an online program at some point.

Now here she was, facing a terrifying job interview with no credentials and only four days to prep. She felt a tinge of guilt as she picked up her phone and texted Jack. "*Hate to do this, but can't make it tonight*," she typed. "*Interview Thursday*."

She added a fingers-crossed emoji, then tossed her phone onto the desk.

She'd felt confident and self-assured after pulling off such a successful wedding, ready to bask in the satisfaction of a job well done.

She was good. She *knew* she was good. Now all she could do was try to swallow the fear of being exposed as a fraud.

Chapter Thirteen

THE HIGHWAY WAS as clear as the cornflower-blue sky overhead as Celeste drove out of Keystone Ridge toward Banff on Thursday morning, but her mind was a jumble of conflicting thoughts.

It was eight in the morning, and she'd had to fake a doctor's appointment to avoid any questions from her family. She didn't want to deal with their input. She was tired of the same refrain: *Of course the new owners will keep you on!* and *They'd be crazy to let you go.* The interview would be a secret, and she'd deal with things later on if by some miracle she ended up getting a job offer.

She glanced at herself in the rearview mirror. At least she appeared put together, with a generous layer of under-eye concealer, her favorite navy Theory suit with a silk sleeveless top underneath, and her grandmother's diamond studs adding a noticeable but discreet touch of elegance. Just the way Celeste liked to operate.

She'd been instructed to park in the employee parking lot at the back of the hotel and report to the hotel's office off to the side of the concierge desk to announce her presence.

The lobby was filled with the sweet scent of the giant fresh floral arrangement sitting in the middle of the high-ceilinged space. A young man in a black suit and close-cropped hair looked up from his concierge desk computer when she approached.

"I'm Celeste McCarthy," she said. "Here to see Stephan Jolliet."

"Welcome, Ms. McCarthy," he said, smiling politely. "Please wait right here." He indicated a leather banquette by the wall that sat underneath a Maud Lewis reproduction. Or, on closer inspection, was it an original? The lobby was immaculately clean, beautifully decorated, and exuded a sense of calm and order.

Celeste sat on the banquette, mindful of her posture, and took a deep breath in, as though she could drink up the serenity and let it unfurl the knots in her stomach. She observed the goings-on at the front desk, the views of the mountains from the windows on one side and the thick forested area spotted with cabins on the other.

A young couple was checking out, moving with the un-hurried, relaxed nature of a successful holiday. Celeste noted how the front desk clerk greeted them promptly with a smile, inquired about their stay, and wished them safe travels home. It wasn't rocket science. So why was she so nervous?

"Ms. McCarthy?" a woman's voice said from beside her. Celeste turned to see the thin-lipped, stern face of Annie Flint, her silver hair pulled back so tight it was a miracle the follicles were holding on. She hadn't known Annie was going to be the one conducting the interview. Wasn't it frowned upon for someone to interview their replacement?

But of course she would. Someone with that strong of an iron grip wouldn't be content to let just *anyone* fill her brushed-leather Prada loafers.

Celeste stood up, smiled politely, and extended her hand to shake Annie's. Every movement, every word, every interaction from this moment on would be judged to see Celeste's manners, her nature, her ability to exude grace under pressure.

"Grayson, please take Ms. McCarthy's jacket." Immediately the young man at the desk relieved her of her coat and disappeared into the back room. "Let's start with a tour, then, shall we?" Annie said, gesturing toward the exit of the lobby. "Stephan will join us in the boardroom after you've had the chance to look around."

"Thank you," said Celeste, and she followed Annie, who strode across the hardwood floors with the precision of a metronome. "What a beautiful place," she said. "The last time I was here, I was twelve. My mom took me for afternoon tea for my birthday. So it's nice to see it again after all these years."

Annie nodded briskly. "Many of our other candidates for the role are international and so won't have the benefit of touring the space. But I think it's important to see what you'd be signing on for. It's not a small operation," she said, dipping her chin as she turned to look at Celeste over her glasses.

Many other candidates? How many was *many*?

Many didn't sound promising.

"This is the guest lounge and bar," Annie said, ushering Celeste into a large multileveled area, with plush velvet seating and a mahogany Bösendorfer grand piano in the middle of the space. She looked up and took in the sight of a stunning chandelier, with clusters of concentrated crystals that extended out in bursts, like a heap of constellations.

"Swarovski, modeled after the New York Metropolitan Opera House," Annie said. "Our owner, Mr. Kantor, is a huge classical-music fan and visits New York, Chicago, or San Francisco one weekend each month. He thought the chandeliers were perfect for the hotel, given the popularity of our observatory."

Celeste had researched the hotel's observatory online, which had a retractable roof and was staffed by a full-time astronomer, making the hotel a magnet for stargazers. The Butterfly Lake Lodge's stargazing room looked like amateur hour in comparison.

Each room was more impressive than the last, and when they finally arrived at the boardroom for the interview, Celeste felt a mixture of awe and nerves. How had she ever thought she would be qualified to manage an operation of this magnitude?

She entered the boardroom to find two people already

sitting at the conference table—a man with white hair and a mustache who introduced himself as Stephan Jolliet and a younger woman with a black bob and thick blue-rimmed glasses.

"I'm Corrine Petersen," she said, "head of HR for The Kantor Group. Water?"

Bless you, thought Celeste. Her throat was dry, and she needed something to do with her hands.

She settled in, and Stephan provided an overview of the role. Then it was her turn.

The first questions were a piece of cake:

Tell us about yourself.

What's the number one most important component of hospitality?

Tell us about a difficult situation you encountered with a guest and how you resolved it.

How do you solicit feedback from your guests to assure continual improvement?

Ten minutes in, she started to relax. Annie had been quiet up until this point, but she noticed the woman began fidgeting in her seat the more Celeste aced the questions.

At a certain point, after Celeste had regaled the panel with a story about the time their towel provider had been late with the delivery and her car had been in the shop, her parents out of town, and she'd taken one of the inn's bicycles forty minutes to the Nordic spa near Canmore and begged to borrow forty towels, balancing them in two large Ikea bags over the handlebars, she had Stephan and Corrine in stitches. But Annie Flint only sat up in her seat and put her elbows on the table, crossing her arms and looking out the window, appearing as disinterested as a house cat.

When she finally piped in, Celeste knew she was going for blood. "Tell us about your experience with PelSIS," Annie said, tapping her pen on the table, then holding it in a poised position, as though she was about to take down a criminal testimony.

Celeste paused. "Well, I noticed on the posting that there was a preference to be well versed in the system. I actually don't—"

"The most well-used hotel management software in the world, and you don't have any experience?" Annie said, raising an eyebrow.

"I'm a fast learner," she said, almost choking.

Annie noted something on the paper in front of her. "Tell us your thoughts about how digitization might impact frontline staff as well as customer experience and what you might do to mitigate any negative effects while also keeping in mind profit maximization."

Celeste paused. Her eyes darted to Corrine and Stephan, neither of whom were making eye contact with her. She felt sick. "I, uh," she said and took a shallow breath in. "I suppose I always think that the human touch far surpasses anything digital. But, um, I'd have to give that some more consideration."

Finally an expression of satisfaction crept over Annie's face, but Celeste suspected it had nothing to do with the quality of her response. "I see on your resume you have an undergraduate degree in…what is it? English literature?" Annie gave her a tight, condescending grin.

"Yes," she squeaked out.

"Have you ever thought of doing your master's? EHL in Switzerland really is the best in the world. I mean, I was there twenty years ago, but it's a fabulous school. You might look into it."

"I'll look it up," Celeste said. Was the interview over? It had all been going so well. Was Annie trying to sabotage her? To expose her as a fraud?

"Uh, I have a couple of more questions," Stephan finally piped up.

"Sure," Celeste said weakly. He asked her to detail how she kept her team motivated, and Corrine informed her of the next stages in the interview process, all while Annie sat back in her seat, her arms crossed, a look of smug satisfaction on her pinched face.

Annie stayed behind in the boardroom while Corrine and Stephan walked her to the front reception, shook her hand, and promised to be in touch.

Celeste waited until she was in the car before cursing out loud.

She hadn't expected it to be a home run, but she also hadn't anticipated being on the hot seat like that.

But most of all, she hadn't expected to be so interested in the job. Initially it had felt like a life raft being thrown her way that she needed to grasp on to. But after touring the beautiful space and considering the new challenges and growth opportunities, she was interested in the role for far more than the mere prospect of continued employment.

Her mind was a mix of tangled wires, and she fought to keep her focus on the road.

Without thinking, instead of taking the exit toward the lodge, Celeste sped past, then took the next off ramp which led down the winding country road toward where Jack told her he lived, in the stretch of homes along the river's bend. The one with the yellow mailbox at the road, he'd said. She didn't allow herself to think too critically about her decision to go there; all she wanted was to see him.

His truck was parked out front when she pulled in, and for a moment she second-guessed her decision. How would he take her coming over unannounced?

She parked her Jeep anyway. She stood on the path, looking at his house, then almost leapt out of her skin as a voice came from behind her. "Celeste?"

She spun around and found Jack with an adorable dog trailing behind him with a tennis ball in his mouth. "Sorry to scare you. We're just coming back from a walk. You're back for another round on the river?" Her face must have still been laced with panic. "Wait, you okay?" he said.

Tears sprung into her eyes unexpectedly, and Jack's expression softened. He put out his arms, and she melted into them, the warm feeling of his strong embrace quieting the nerves and doubt that laced through her. She breathed in the smell of his jacket, earthy mixed with the spice of aftershave, and steadied herself.

"You had your interview today, didn't you?" he said, pulling back and studying her face. "Come on in. Tell me how it went."

Jack made coffee while Celeste sat on his couch, petting Bodie, who kept his head in her lap, looking up at her with a tender, innocent gaze. "He likes you," Jack said. He brought the mugs of coffee over and deposited one on the table.

"I guess this is why these guys are used as therapy pets," she said.

"He's attuned to how people are feeling, that's for sure." Jack sat in the spot next to her and rubbed the spot behind Bodie's ears. "So. Talk to me."

"Sorry to just barge in like this," Celeste said. She took a sip of her coffee.

"It's all right," he said. "To be honest, I was wondering if I'd hear from you. After you missing class."

Celeste shifted in her seat. "I know. It's just—there's been a lot going on."

"Okay. You going to tell me about it?"

"I wasn't sure about this interview. I mean, I didn't really even want to apply in the first place. And I thought I was prepared. But then I got there and the place is stunning and

I think I could do a really good job."

"So, what's the problem, then?"

"The problem is that I was made to look like a complete fool by Annie Flint. She's the one vacating the job. And it was like she was out to get me the whole interview."

"She probably realizes you're going to do a better job. And she can't handle it."

"Well, I walked out of there feeling like a complete idiot." She felt her voice waver and willed herself not to cry.

"So, call them back. Tell them you want another chance, without her there."

Celeste shook her head. "I can't do that. I just have to keep my eye out for another job." She put her head back on the couch. "Ugh."

"Can I make a suggestion?" His voice was gentle and reassuring.

"Sure."

"Given that you still have your job, a job that you love, and you don't know for sure that you won't have that job for the time being…"

"I can't live with that kind of uncertainty," she confessed, her voice barely above a whisper.

He leaned in closer, his gaze intense yet comforting. "What's the fun in that?" His words held a challenge, a spark of mischief dancing in his eyes.

"It's kind of my thing."

"What do you mean?"

"My whole job is to anticipate what's next. What time the honeymooners will be down for breakfast and whether they'll want Bloody Marys or mimosas. If the temperature is going to drop early in the season and we need to make sure the firewood is well stocked. You know—customer service?"

Jack looked at her with a funny look. "Now that you say it, it makes sense. And you're damn good at it. But does that mean you have to live your entire life that way? Not leaving anything to chance or having a little faith that things will work out as they should?"

"You make me sound so rigid."

Jack set down his coffee cup and turned to fully face her. "That's not what I meant."

But Celeste knew he was right. She liked predictability, order. There was elegance in a well-executed plan, but Jack brought forth something wild inside her, longing to break free. She managed a tight grin.

"There's nothing wrong with having a plan. That wasn't what I meant. All I'm saying is that it seems to me like you don't need to be panicking at this point. And"—he fixed her in his gaze—"I'm sure you knocked the interview out of the park."

Celeste wasn't feeling despondent anymore. With Jack's soothing words, the steady, reassuring comfort of his solidness beside her, not only did she feel protected, but the wave of desire that washed over her erased any self-doubt and concern for anything too far in the future.

She was in the moment, so alive and present and turned on. Was it time to do something completely impulsive?

"Thank you," she said quietly, her voice barely a whisper but filled with anticipation. She put her hand over his on the couch, a silent invitation hanging in the air between them. He took the invitation and leaned over, his lips covering hers. She kissed him, feeling his hands gently pulling her onto his lap.

Celeste melted into Jack's embrace, savoring the warmth of his body against hers, his hands wandering to the small of her back, pulling her closer until there was no space left between them.

Their kiss deepened, becoming more urgent, hungry. When Jack started to trail kisses down her neck and along her collarbone, a soft moan escaped her lips. "I want you," she whispered into his ear. He said nothing before scooping her up into his arms and carrying her to his room.

Chapter Fourteen

"DO YOU REALLY have to go?" Jack said, lacing a finger through the belt loop of the pants she'd just pulled on and tugging her slightly toward him. He was still lying back in bed, a place she would've been very happy to spend the rest of the day, but she'd already be way later getting back to the lodge than she'd said she'd be.

Celeste allowed him to pull her close, and she closed her eyes as he kissed her again, softly this time, a perfect bookend to all of the other incredible ways he'd touched her over the past hour, making her forget all about the disastrous interview, the worries and insecurities melting away under his focused, wanting attention.

She felt her willpower crumbling, until she saw her phone lighting up from inside her purse on the floor. She had to go. "I should have been back at the lodge hours ago. People are probably wondering if I drove off the road or something."

Jack followed her out to the entrance, where she slipped on her shoes and her jacket. He had pulled on his jeans, but his shirt was still on the floor in his room. Seeing his broad, sculpted torso in the bright light of the living room made leaving feel all but impossible.

She turned to him before leaving. Jack circled her waist and pulled her against him, his hair ruffled and his gaze still filled with desire. She closed her eyes as he kissed the nape of her neck again ever so slowly. He knew how to get to her. "All right. Call me later."

Call me later. Those three simple words. Not an expression of any kind of feeling, necessarily, but the kind of thing you said to someone when what was happening between you wasn't a one-time event. Was Jack going to be more than a one-time event?

He was an amazing man, and she was falling for him.

She would call him later.

Jack walked her to her car and stood outside as she drove back to the highway, her entire body buzzing with satisfaction.

She slid her phone out of her purse to see who'd called minutes earlier. Her stomach dropped when she looked at her home screen and saw the notification for nine missed calls, all from the lodge.

Something terrible had happened. There were no texts and no voicemails.

Celeste dialed the lodge's number, set the call to hands-free, and all but sped away from Jack's house to the highway, her heart trying to escape her chest.

When no one picked up, she was tempted to hit the gas

pedal harder, but this highway was always teeming with speed patrol. She took a deep, steadying breath.

She pulled into the lodge and ran up the back path and let herself in the door.

Her parents were both sitting at the kitchen island, looking unconcerned if only a little confused at how she'd burst through the door.

"What's wrong?" she said.

"Nothing. What—"

"I wanted to ask where you'd left my purple sweater," said Quinn from behind her. "What's wrong with you?"

"You called me nine times!" she hissed.

"I really wanted to wear it to coffee with Jasmine. You said your appointment was over at ten."

Celeste took a steadying breath. "Why didn't you text? Or leave a message?"

"Jeez," said Quinn, holding her hands up. "I'm sorry. I thought you were driving."

She closed her eyes, willing herself not to bite off her sister's head. What would Quinn say if she knew that only an hour ago, she'd been under the sheets at Jack's house, thinking of anything but Quinn and her purple sweater?

"Forget it," Celeste mumbled. "I'll be in my office."

She shut the door and sat in her chair and stared at the wall. Maybe it would be better to move on from the lodge. Living and working so closely with her family might not have been the healthiest, the most conducive for her to live an adult life.

Or maybe impulsivity just wasn't her thing.

"SORRY TO HEAR that," Jack said, flipping open his organizer and running his finger across the calendar until he found May twenty-second, the date he was supposed to host a youth group from a community center in Nanaimo. They'd just called to cancel, citing a budget shortfall for the year. "What if I knock 10 percent off the price?"

"No can do," said the woman on the other end. "Our funding wasn't approved by council this year, so the only trip we'll be doing is to the local park."

"All right," Jack said. "Hope we'll see you in the future." He pressed End on his home screen, then tossed his phone across the table and leaned back in his chair, grunting. It was the second cancellation he'd had in under a week, the other a local outdoorsmen club that called to see if he'd price match, of all companies, Forrest Outfitters. He had half a mind to tell the guy all about Forrest, but at the time he'd thought *Screw 'em.* Had he known this other group was going to pull out, he might have acted differently.

He flipped open his laptop and navigated to the back end of the reservations section of his website, where he added a limited-time-offer discount on any booking for the end of the month, then made a post on Instagram to advertise it.

"Come on, Bodie," he said and whistled. He was frustrated and annoyed and needed to blow off some steam.

The early-evening sunshine was streaming through the trees, lighting up the worn path through the woods that Jack knew like the back of his hand.

Bodie sniffed around, and Jack took some deep breaths of the calm, cool air. He felt for his phone in his pocket. What was Celeste up to tonight? It was Friday, so maybe she'd be available to go out for dinner.

Their afternoon together the day before still felt like a dream, and if it was, he had no interest in waking up from it. That determined glint in her eyes as she'd closed the distance between them, her movements filled with confidence. The fragility he had seen moments before had melted away to a quiet strength that had taken his breath away.

He could still feel her fingers tracing the contours of his jawline before she'd leaned in, her lips meeting his in a passionate kiss that had left him reeling.

He wanted more. The physical piece, for sure. But he was interested in that and so much more. For a second, he had a flash in his mind of them sitting on the couch together, her feet on his lap and Bodie on the floor in front of them, a movie on and the fireplace going.

Maybe he'd drop by the lodge after work and bring by the pamphlets she'd invited him to put out at the front desk. If she was free, he'd invite her to dinner.

Jack could *see* himself with Celeste, a future he hadn't

envisioned in a very long time.

AFTER DROPPING BODIE off, Jack packed his gear, then drove to the Bow River meeting spot to meet the day's group. There was a family of four from Dallas, a couple from Ottawa, and two students from UBC's forestry program who were taking a break from a field-research project in the area.

It was a good group—all beginners but they asked lots of questions, and after a couple of hours, one of the UBC students had the first catch, which seemed to give confidence to the rest of the group, who, one by one, were able to reel in a catch of their own.

They were just starting to clear out of the river when Jack spotted Forrest's Hummer turn into the parking area, followed by a black Land Rover.

Jack cursed under his breath. Clearly Forrest hadn't gotten the message the other day. If it weren't for the fact that his clients were there, he'd have charged right over to him and told him what's what.

He helped his group out of their waders and watched out of the corner of his eye as Forrest outfitted three middle-aged men from the Land Rover, then led them down to the river.

At least this time he'd brought them farther away from Jack's space, but it wasn't an area Jack would have recommended. The water was deeper and there was a section with a strong current, so despite it being on the more dangerous side, it was just a plain stupid place to bring someone to catch a fish, regardless of their experience.

"That was great," said the mother of the family from Dallas. "Our friends are coming this way later in the summer. I'll pass along your number."

"Appreciate that," said Jack. He eyed the decals on the side of the Hummer, which also detailed Forrest's website. "Tell them to mention you sent them and I'll knock 15 percent off the price." At this rate, he'd be operating at a loss. But it would be worth it just to keep people from booking with Forrest.

After Jack saw off the rest of the group, he spent some time cleaning his equipment by the river and organizing the tackle boxes.

He was about to get into his truck when shouting came from the water. He left the door of his truck door open and jogged down to the river's edge to get a better view.

One of the men was on his back, struggling to stand up. Forrest was racing toward him, but running through the water wasn't easy and the man continued to struggle as the river's current carried him away from the group.

Jack stood watching for a split second, mind calculating the best response. He ran back to his truck, fired up the engine, and executed a quick three-point-turn, then barreled down the gravel path in the direction of the river's flow. He had to travel faster than the current was taking the man.

He scanned the river ahead as he drove, then pinpointed a spot he knew was on the shallower side. When he was as close as he could get with the truck, he threw the gear shift into Park and leapt out. There was only one place he had a chance of saving the man before the river swept him farther out to the wide basin where it would be impossible to intervene.

Heart pounding in his chest, he ran down to the riverbank. He could see the man, still caught in the current and struggling to right himself. At this point, his waders would be so full of water that it would be all but impossible.

Jack kept his eyes on a semi-shallow area with a fallen tree he could use to hang on to.

About one hundred meters away, he watched the man try to stand up again, then get knocked over by the force of the rushing river. The rocks were slippery, and unless you had tremendous lower-body strength, it would be all but impossible to save yourself, especially when you threw fear into the mix. Knocking your head against a rock was no small threat either.

Holding on to the tree for support, Jack waded in, trying to calculate the best place to stand based on the currents he could see rippling through the water. The branch only extended so far, so he said a silent prayer that he'd be strong enough to continue.

Without his waders, the cold water shot daggers of ice through his skin, and his Blundstones were weighed down like anchors as he tried to move toward the path he predicted the man would take.

Jack approached the spot when all of a sudden, the tree branch gave way and disappeared through the current with the strength of the water. He stumbled into the river, catching his fall against a sharp rock. Blood started to flow from the palm of his hand down his wrist.

He had about ten seconds to intercept the fisher. There was no way he was letting the man get washed by; it was certain death.

In a semi-crouched position, he engaged every muscle in his lower body and continued taking small steps forward, keeping his eye on the moving target rushing toward him.

For a moment, it looked like he wasn't going to make it in time, but a larger boulder ahead allowed him to raise himself up to the surface water, reach out, and grab the collar of the man's shirt.

"Hang on," he said, passing the man his other hand. "I need you to try to stand up."

The man's eyes were filled with fear, but after a few seconds and with Jack's assistance, he managed to get himself upright again.

"Now put your arm around my shoulder. We're going to walk back together."

Jack and the man moved slowly as a pair back to land, where Forrest and the other two men were standing. Forrest waded in as soon as they were almost back to shore. "All good!" he called, as though he hadn't almost just seen a client washed away under his idiocy.

The man's friends helped him onto the riverbank, and Jack took a few steps away from the group to catch his breath.

Forrest joined him immediately. "Thanks, man," he said. "That was some quick thinking."

Jack glared at him. "You know you almost killed him, right?" he said in a hushed voice. "What were you doing, taking them into such a fast spot?"

"I've taken plenty of groups there," Forrest said. His expression had changed from panicked to defensive.

"Well, you must have a horseshoe up your ass or something. I can't believe this hasn't happened yet."

Forrest glanced over at his group, then back at him. "Thanks for your help," he said. "I'd better get back to them."

"Don't do anything stupid like that again," Jack said. "Gives all of us a bad name. Even those of us who know what they're doing."

Without waiting for a response, he made his way up to the path lining the river's edge that would lead him back to his truck, wet boots squelching on the gravel.

He shook his head as he slammed the door to his truck, then turned on the ignition.

The only bright side to being soaked head to toe with a bleeding hand was knowing that idiot was about to get his first one-star review.

"I've got Janice coming at eight tomorrow morning. She's our best," Celeste said, smiling at the husband and wife who'd come to the front desk to book a massage appointment for the wife the next morning. "Is there anything I can arrange for you, sir?"

"Just another delivery of those cinnamon buns!" he said, patting his stomach. "I'll be happy to sit back with one of those and my coffee while she has her massage."

"Excellent. Well, if there's anything else you need, you know where to find me."

The couple made their way to the staircase to their second-floor suite, and Celeste moved back to the office and checked her phone. She warmed when she saw a message from Jack, asking if he could come by to drop off some materials for their pamphlet display, goose bumps forming at the thought of being near him again.

Just as she was about to reply, her phone started to vibrate in her hand with a call coming through. When she saw the name of the screen, her heart skipped a beat. She took a deep breath in. "Hello?"

A deep voice came through the phone. "Celeste, this is Stephan Jolliet calling from the Keystone Ridge Resort."

Celeste grimaced. His voice was laced with bad news. "Yes," she said. "Hello, Stephan. How are you?"

"I'm well—thank you. We appreciate you coming in yesterday. Celeste, the reason for my call is that I'm speaking on behalf of the team here to say we were really impressed with your interview. But…" he said and hesitated.

But what we actually think is that you had no business applying for this job, she predicted and squeezed her eyes shut, ready to absorb the blow.

"We did have another internal candidate apply from one of our partner hotels in the US and have offered him the job."

"I appreciate you calling," Celeste said. She knew she would be disappointed, but what she hadn't anticipated was the contradictory sense of relief. She wasn't ready to take on a job of that scope. She needed more experience. She needed to go back to school. She needed—

"We have another opportunity to offer you, however," he said. "It's…a bit different. But we think you're up for the challenge, with your experience at a smaller property. We're opening a boutique resort on Lagoon Island, just off the northeast side of Vancouver Island. You would be part of the team leading the opening. Helping to train the staff. Establishing systems. It's a short-term contract with the possibility of extending, if we're happy with your work."

Celeste was speechless. "Thank you," she said. "I—"

"We'd like to invite you for a site visit. It will need to be early next week, though. We're eager to move forward on this, so we'll need your decision as soon as possible. I'll have my assistant make arrangements for you."

Early next week? The lodge had a number of bookings, an art show opening in the gallery, and the pub was hosting a trivia night. She'd barely have time to think, never mind leave for an island hours away.

"I'll need to think about it," she heard herself say, butter-flies doing whatever was the butterfly version of a cartwheel in her stomach. "Can I call you by the end of the weekend to confirm?"

The other end of the line was silent for a beat. "We really are eager to get plans in place. Please let me know by Sunday at the latest."

"I'll speak with you then," Celeste said. Her nerves quickly morphed to excitement as the details of the conversation settled. Lagoon Island. It sounded kind of dreamy.

She opened the map app on her phone and input the island's name to calculate the distance from Keystone Ridge, then grimaced when the app couldn't calculate a route. She zoomed out from the map, the vast distance between it and her home staring back at her. The vast distance between her and Jack.

Her mind whirled. Okay, so it was far away. But it wasn't on the other side of the world. Ava managed to get home when she could, and Celeste would have two days a week off.

If it was real, this thing between her and Jack, they'd make it work.

HALF AN HOUR later, Jack had changed out of his wet clothes and packed away the rest of his gear.

He glanced at the clock on his dashboard as he approached town. It was just before six and most of the shops would be closing soon, but he only needed to make a quick stop.

The shop attendant at Petal Pusher was pulling in the sandwich board in front of the store. "Mind if I grab something real quick?" Jack asked the young woman.

"Sure thing," she said. He held the door open for her, then followed her inside the small shop, which was filled with an earthy warm smell and buckets of all kinds of different flowers. He scanned the selection and felt pressure to pick quickly, to let the attendant get on with her night, but there was too much to choose from.

"Who are they for, and what's the occasion?"

"Uh, a woman, and no occasion, really," he said.

"Give me five minutes," she said. "I'll put something nice together."

As he stood waiting for the bouquet, he glanced at the community bulletin board to the side of the cash register. A flier caught his eye, with an image of a man and a woman in a float boat, the woman pulling a catch out of the water with a smile plastered across her face. *Special introductory price*, said the text across the top of the page. He read on to see that the flier was advertising yet another new outdoor-adventure company in the area.

Was no one doing market research? Or was he just bleeding dry for the benefit of all these new startups?

He had to figure out something, fast, before these new operations wiped him off the map completely.

"Here you are," the florist said. "What do you think?"

"Great," he said and handed over his credit card, knowing full well he was buying flowers for a woman he wouldn't be able to afford to date soon.

ON THE SHORT drive over to the lodge, Jack played through a few scenarios in his head. Hopefully Celeste would be the one to greet him at the front desk. How would he explain the flowers to her parents or her sister? He knew one thing she found challenging about working at the lodge was that her whole family knew her business.

Showing up here with flowers was probably inappropriate. But the idea of going another day without seeing Celeste didn't feel like an option. He missed her badly, and besides, she'd invited him to drop off his marketing materials.

He would leave the flowers on the front seat just in case. Hopefully she was available for dinner.

He pulled into the lodge parking lot and brought his truck to a stop beside Celeste's Jeep and flipped down his visor to check his hair in the mirror. It was time for a haircut. He pulled on his ballcap, grabbed the envelope of pamphlets and scaled the front steps of the lodge, then paused for a moment before entering, peering through the window to see what was going on in the reception area.

Bingo. Celeste was alone, standing at the desk working on her laptop. His heart swelled. She looked focused on whatever she was doing, her hair pulled back into a ponytail and lower lip jutting out a bit as she leaned in to examine something on her screen. She'd done this in class when she'd been concentrating. It was adorable.

Jack pushed the heavy wooden door open, and Celeste glanced up as he entered. Surprise registered, then a grin spread across her face. For a second, he could see it. Coming home to Celeste, to her sparkling smile and warm energy. The touch of her lips. Falling asleep with her in his arms.

"Hey," Celeste said. She flipped her laptop lid half-closed, then emerged from behind the desk. "This is a nice surprise."

The emerald-green dress she was wearing matched her eyes and hugged her body in a way that conjured images in his mind from the day before. He cleared his throat. "Just thought I'd bring these pamphlets by. Thanks for offering to put them out."

"Of course," she said. She took the stack from the envelope, and he watched as she made room for them in the wooden display at the side of the reception desk. "I'm giving you the most prominent spot. People take these all the time."

"Thanks," said Jack. "Appreciate it."

Celeste tossed the empty manila envelope onto the front desk. She looked at her watch. "Come on in. Can you stay for a few minutes?"

"Actually, I was wondering if you wanted to go for a bite to eat or something. We could walk into town. It's pretty nice out."

She looked behind her. "I heard some footsteps upstairs a few minutes ago. Happy hour's still going for another thirty minutes, so I should probably stick around. But can I get you a drink or something? I have some exciting news to tell you."

He wasn't sure he could take much more excitement than he was feeling, fighting the urge to reach out and take a hold of her hand, pull her close and kiss her the way he had the other day, when the small moan that had escaped her mouth had taken him to a place he'd never been before. But he could be patient. "Oh yeah?" Jack said. "What's that?"

"I would have texted you, but I wanted to tell you in person. So, this is perfect." Her eyes sparkled with excitement. "I got a call from the Keystone Ridge Resort!"

"That's incredible," Jack said. He wasn't at all surprised, but she'd been doubting herself, and this was important to her. He opened his arms and wrapped her in a big hug, drawing in a long breath as he kissed the top of her head, basking in her soft floral scent and the feeling of her body under the silky fabric of her dress.

He pulled back and grinned at her. "You got the job?" His mind raced, considering what he could do to help her celebrate. He could take her somewhere nice, maybe an overnight at a nice place in Yoho. No distractions. No family around. Just him and Celeste and some time to indulge in each other.

"No," she said. She ran her hand down the edge of his open jacket, then slid her arm around his waist. He wanted nothing more than to take her somewhere they could be alone. "But they offered me something else." She looked up at him with a bright smile.

He loved seeing her excited like this. "And what's that?"

She took a deep breath. "I still don't know what to think about it, but it could be great. It's a brand-new resort they've built off Port Hardy. It's super remote. Which, I know, what am I going to do in the middle of nowhere, right? But at least there's a spa, so manicures are available."

Celeste kept talking, but all Jack could focus on was the same gut punch he'd experienced when Christine had told him she was leaving him. His mind whirled with what Celeste was telling him as he struggled to maintain a steady facial expression.

He watched as the bright light in her eyes dimmed and her smile turned down a little. "What?"

Jack's mind raced. She was expecting congratulations and for him to be happy, though he felt anything but. "What do you mean, what?"

"That look on your face." She stepped back, searching his expression.

Jack dug deep but couldn't do it. "I don't know what you—"

He stopped when a young couple appeared at the foot of the staircase, two men holding hands and seemingly aware they were interrupting a private moment. "We're sorry to intrude," said one of the men. "But any chance we could order a bottle of wine in front of the fire?"

"And if you have any more of those pretzel bites..." the other man said.

"Of course," said Celeste. "The wine menu is on the table. Please have a look, and I'll be there shortly." The men disappeared to the great room, and she looked back at Jack, confusion in her eyes. "Can you stick around for a few minutes?" she said.

And what? Hear all about the job that was going to take her to a remote area of a different province? "Ah, no, I've gotta get back. Bodie needs a walk," he said. He zipped up his jacket all the way and made for the door.

"Wait," Celeste said quietly.

The insistence in her voice almost stopped him in his tracks, but he needed out. Jack reached for the door handle. "You go ahead—I know you're busy," he said.

He paused before opening the door. He shouldn't leave like this. But he didn't know what else to do.

The only sound was the soft classical music playing through the lodge's speaker system.

"Jack," said Celeste. "I thought you'd be happy for me. You encouraged me to do this." Her expression was pleading. It was too much.

"I am happy for you," he said, almost choking on his words. He knew he was being unfair. He had encouraged her. He'd hoped for her to get good news. But the truth was his buy-in had a limit. Now she was leaving, and he'd be the left-behind all over again. He felt pathetic. He couldn't be that guy.

"Listen," he said. He could barely force himself to make eye contact with her, and when he did, the hurt in her deep green eyes hit him like a dagger. "I think you're great. But this isn't going to work out."

Her concern turned to annoyance. "You told me I should go for it."

"I'm happy for you," he said, but no one with a brain would have believed him.

She took a deep breath, then exhaled. "Well, you're doing a shitty job at showing it."

They stood in silence, until Jack reached into his pocket and pulled out his keys. He had two choices: Let Celeste know how much she meant to him and pretend they could make it work long distance, only for her to fade away. Or just cut to the inevitable.

He didn't want any part in her staying behind. This was

her life, and if she stayed and things didn't work out with them, or if, like she was predicting, the lodge changed hands to someone who wasn't prepared to employ her, she'd just resent him for it. It was best for them both to just move on.

"You're right," he said. "You deserve better. 'Night, Celeste."

She didn't follow him out, and he didn't blame her.

He got into the truck and glanced at the bouquet of flowers on the passenger seat and shook his head, then turned on the ignition, a wave of foolishness washing over him. He'd let it happen again, but this time was worse.

This time he'd known better.

Chapter Fifteen

"GO AWAY," CELESTE said, burrowing farther under a quilt on the couch in her living room after another set of knocks came at her door. Quinn had been by twice already since she'd told her parents she couldn't work that day, and Celeste had been forced to tell her what had happened with Jack. Quinn had tried to give her advice, but after a few minutes she'd told her sister she just wanted to be alone. Quinn was sweet. She was a great listener. But she had never been in love, and Celeste didn't feel like talking to someone who didn't get it.

She heard the door open. "Sorry, not sorry," a voice called—the most perfect of voices for what she was feeling right now. It was Ava.

Celeste sat up as she came through the door, her arms weighed down by bags.

"Holy hell, you look like shit," Ava said. She laughed. "Clearly I should have been here hours ago!"

Celeste burst into tears, burying her head in the pillow.

Ava approached the couch, dropped the bags she was holding, and sat right next to her, taking Celeste's head in her hands. "Get a grip, Celeste," she said. "And once you've done that, go get ready. We're going out tonight."

"I'm not going anywhere," she said.

"I gave up a full day with Sam to come up here. She's with Calista overnight. I dropped over a grand on a great outfit for you—and under-eye patches, which I thought you might need." She ripped the pillow away from under her head and examined Celeste's face. "I was right. So you," she said, pressing her finger to Celeste's chest, which made her laugh, despite herself, "are getting your ass in the shower while I mix us some negronis and warm up these patties from Steady's."

Celeste's eyes pooled with tears again. "I love you," she said. She buried her head in her sister's shoulder.

Ava took her by the shoulders and looked at her head on. "Stop emoting. Go get ready," she said.

Celeste stood under the hot stream of water in the shower. The last thing she wanted to do was go anywhere, but she wouldn't win with Ava. One drink at home, one at the bar, and in a couple of hours, she'd be changing back into her fleece pajamas and crawling into bed, floating off to a dream world where Jack Wallace didn't exist.

When she exited the shower, she found a wardrobe bag on her bed. Ava might not have been the one she could count on for warm fuzzies, but she was thoughtful and showed love in her own way.

And today she was showing her love with a very generous

swipe of her credit card. Celeste's eyes widened as she pulled out a soft knit off-white cashmere sweater dress from the Holt Renfrew bag, with a price tag that left no doubt her sister was doing very well at her job.

She slid the dress over her body and looked in the mirror. It fit her perfectly, and for something on the more snug side, it was also very comfortable. Maybe money did buy happiness.

When she returned to the kitchen, Ava had laid out some bowls of appetizers and two deep-orange cocktails. She looked up at Celeste and nodded in approval. "Much better," she said. "Where do you want to go tonight?"

Back to the couch? she thought. "Maybe Allen's?" Celeste said. It was just far enough out of town that they likely wouldn't run into anyone they knew.

She noted Ava's lips purse slightly. "Not Allen's," she said. "Let's just go into town. I don't want to drive." The way Ava flinched at the mention of the popular nightspot was a bit strange, but Celeste didn't argue. If they ended up running into old friends, at least she could leave Ava behind and not have to worry about a ride.

They walked through the wooded path into town, which took them a bit out of the way, but walking at the side of the highway at night, where there was only a gravel shoulder, was a bad idea, especially after a drink or two.

Best Case Brewery was on Keystone Ridge's main strip and was operated by two former lawyers and best friends who'd left the profession to pursue their other dream. The brewery served several different types of beer but also had a great cocktail menu and, apparently, poured shots.

"Thanks," Ava said, sliding her credit card across the bar to the young bartender. "I'll start a tab."

"Seriously?" Celeste said, trailing her sister to a high-top table near the window. "Shots? What are we, twenty-three years old?"

"I never get to go out anymore," Ava said. She placed the shot glasses on the table, shrugged off her jacket, and slung it over her stool, then nodded at the table. "It's Saturday night. Indulge me." Ava held up her shot glass to clink against Celeste's.

She tipped her head back, then grimaced as the tequila burned the back of her throat. "Ugh. Tequila will forever remind me of Jordan Randall's party in grade twelve."

Ava laughed. "How many weeks were we grounded for that summer?"

"At least three for me. Maybe only two for you." Celeste had broken the rules very few times in her life, but when she had, she'd made it count. Ava had only been fifteen at the time and begged Celeste to bring her with her. She had refused until Ava had threatened to spill to their parents about the blow-out party, and she'd begrudgingly brought her sister along.

Another girl at the party had given Celeste a dirty look for talking to her boyfriend, and Ava had sloshed her cheap beer in the girl's face and threatened to rip her ponytail extension off.

Maybe it was the tequila, but Celeste's heart warmed at the thought of her sister going to bat for her like that. Ava was tough. She was complicated. But she was so fiercely loyal, and the fact that she'd driven all the way from the city to take Celeste out meant a lot. She took a deep breath and decided to go all in. "Next shot's on me. Then Robyn or Sia?"

Ava's face lit up and a devilish smile crossed her face. "Now we're talking."

Celeste collected two more shots from the bar and held them in the spaces between her pointer and middle fingers and middle and ring fingers as she leaned over to request a song from the DJ, who looked like he'd just walked out of his high school exams, then returned to the table to join her sister.

"Speaking of talking…"

Celeste waited. Ava wasn't a talker, but she sensed her sister had dragged her out to do more than drink.

"Okay?" Celeste said.

"Quinn told me she found you in the office in tears last night."

"Yeah," Celeste said. She stared at the coaster on the table and scraped at the edges of it with her thumbnail.

"Want to tell me what that's all about?"

"Not really."

"Come on."

Celeste looked at her sister pointedly. "That's pretty rich coming from you, the world's most secretive person."

Ava leaned in. "Except I know you want to talk."

Celeste sighed. She did, actually, although she was worried about getting all teary in such a public place, where she recognized at least half of the other guests. "Fine. I'll tell you what happened, but I don't want to talk about it, okay?" Ava nodded. "I think I really screwed things up with Jack. He's been so supportive and so there for me, and I didn't even think about the fact that my leaving town would be a dealbreaker."

"Leaving town?" Ava said.

"I got a job offer in BC."

Her sister raised an eyebrow. "I'm assuming you haven't told Mom and Dad."

"No. And don't say anything. I'm going to tell them tomorrow."

"I won't." She paused. "And Jack didn't jump up and down at the news. Celeste, come on, what did you expect?"

Celeste felt her throat constrict. "I don't know. The job was a total surprise. And I guess I just thought if it was real, we'd make it work."

"That's a really long way away. Especially for a new relationship."

She took a sip of her drink. "I think I ruined everything."

"And you've fallen for him," Ava said softly.

Celeste swallowed. "Yeah."

"Is this new job… Is this what you really want?"

Celeste shook her head. "I don't know. But I put myself second before—with Matt. I don't want to do that again."

"I can respect that," said Ava.

They sat for a moment in silence as the lanky twentysomething host of the karaoke night took the mic.

"*Lllladies* and gentlemen, welcome to Best Case Brewery's karaoke night!" he called. "Write down your song from *A* to *Z*; it's time to let those vocals free. This is not a night of competition, just a place of musical ignition!"

Celeste looked at Ava and rolled her eyes. "This could be bad." She did, however, remember a few of the lodge's guests coming back after a night at the brewery remarking on "decent local talent."

The host read out instructions for signups, then launched into "Kiss from a Rose." He had a good voice, as far as talent went in the Keystone Ridge area.

A red-haired woman in her early fifties was up next and did a pretty decent job with "We Belong Together" by Mariah Carey, and by the time she got to the chorus, Celeste nodded to the door. "I'm out," she said. "What is this, the heartbreak hotel?"

"Lyrics just hit you differently when you're hurting," Ava said with authority. Celeste found it very hard to believe anyone had ever hurt Ava. But maybe she was wrong. "Stay here," Ava said, hopping off her stool.

Celeste watched as her sister strode to the bar, then picked up her phone, hoping that maybe Jack had texted, but the only message that had come through was a reminder from her hairdresser that she had an appointment scheduled in the morning.

Ava slid back into her seat moments later and slid a rocks glass across the table. "Drink that. We're up next."

"Forget it!" Celeste said. She stood up and looked around for her coat, but it had disappeared from the hook beside their table. "Where's my coat?"

"I hid it," her sister said, a look of mischief in her eyes.

"Give it to me. My keys are in it. I'm going home."

"Exactly," Ava said. "I'll give you your keys after you sing a song with me."

"Fine. I'll stay at Mom and Dad's."

Ava leaned in, grabbed Celeste's chin, and looked her straight in the eyes. "Veruca Salt."

Celeste shook her head free from her sister's grip. "You're using it on *this*?"

Ava nodded, a small smile threatening to spill. "Yup."

Years ago, on Quinn's sixteenth birthday, when Quinn had begged them all to go to the local pioneer village and participate in a historical reenactment of a town-hall debate, costumes included, they'd begrudgingly agreed but only after making it clear to Quinn she'd used up her one trump card. "Volcano Girls" by Veruca Salt had been playing on the radio in the car on the way over, so they'd used the band's name to coin the phrase they could use when they wanted to veto a decision, a one-and-done card they could play. And now it seemed Ava was cashing hers in.

"You're evil. Are you kidding me right now?"

"Drink up," Ava said as the host took to the mic.

"Calling up Celeste and Ava," he said, and there was a smattering of applause through the room.

Before she could protest, Ava linked her arm in Celeste's, picked up both of their drinks, and seconds later Celeste was standing on stage with a blinding bright spotlight on them.

Ava shoved a mic into one of her hands and her drink in the other, just as the opening chords of the most outrageous karaoke song Celeste could think of came through the speakers.

"Wait, this is the wrong—"

"Nope! It's right," Ava yelled gleefully in her ear over the music. "No love songs, right? Let's alternate *yeah*s. Then you've got the first verse. Take it to the chorus."

It was a good thing Celeste, Ava, and Elodie had spent much of their teen years choreographing dances, with Quinn and her stuffies as their audience, because Celeste barely had to look at the screen for lyrics.

The drinks had done their job, because Celeste was no longer feeling any iota of stage fright. In fact, with her new outfit and the confidence that came with having Ava beside her, she suddenly felt like a pop star, ready to tell the rest of the pub to *ride it, my pony*. Ginuwine would be proud!

They sang. They danced, back to back and perhaps a little more raunchily than the Best Case Brewery karaoke crowd was used to. They laughed. The crowd cheered, although the room might have been echoey, but Celeste decided that she and Ava were just that talented. So much so that a few patrons had their cameras up, recording them. She was too drunk to care!

They stepped off the stage, bent over laughing. "Let's do another!" Celeste proclaimed, stumbling and catching herself on a couple's table and sloshing their drinks. "Sorry!" she proclaimed. Ava signaled to the bar for another round. "Let's do Robyn!" Celeste said. She *loved* Robyn. And the pub would *love* them singing it! *Tralala!*

"One more, then home," Ava said, and Celeste loved her sister even more than she ever had before.

THE NEXT MORNING, when Celeste woke up in a fully incapacitating nausea, a brick taking up space in her skull, and the foul remnants of ethanol in her mouth, she loved her sister much less.

By some kind of miracle, they only had three rooms booked at the lodge, so there was minimal work to do before she dragged herself to the salon, where the scent of hair dye and the warmth of the hair dryer were almost too much to bear, and even when she stepped out with a fresh cut, dye, and blowout, when she looked at the rearview mirror of her car, she still looked rough.

The only thing she could think about was Miss Vickie's jalapeño chips, which usually did the trick, so on her way back to the lodge, she pulled into the parking lot near the IGA in Banff.

Under the bright fluorescent lights of the grocery store, she grabbed the chips and a bottle of Perrier and brought them to the checkout. The cashier blinked at her. "Great job last night," she said, then grinned.

"Oh no. You were at Best Case?" Celeste said. She tapped her debit card on the machine, and then the girl passed her the receipt. From what she could remember, there had been around thirty to forty people there, and hopefully most of them were out-of-towners who she'd never see again.

The young woman cocked her head to the side and peered at her through her red-rimmed glasses. "No, I saw it on Keystone Konnection. I'm only eighteen."

Celeste almost dropped the bottle. "You what?"

"I'm only eighteen. Everyone tells me I look older."

"No, I'm asking about the video. What do you mean you saw something on Keystone Konnection?"

"There's a video of you. And another girl, singing. Dancing. Looks like it was a great time."

After mumbling something about peer pressure and alcohol, Celeste raced back to her car, threw the water and chips onto the passenger seat, and opened the Instagram app on her phone. Trying her best to steady the now-raging nausea, she navigated to the account that reposted anything that was tagged *Keystone Ridge*. Her stomach lurched when she saw a shaky video of her on stage, doing her very best Ginuwine impression, her provocative grinding nowhere near as impressive as it had been in her mind the night before.

Everyone would see it. Her friends. Her parents.

Jack.

Ugh. She slunk down in her seat and squeezed her eyes shut, the wave of embarrassment and regret colliding with her hangover in a perfect storm.

She took a deep, steadying breath, then replayed the video. How many people did she know that followed this account? Certainly everyone in Keystone Ridge. And probably the surrounding area.

Including Annie Flint.

WHEN SHE RETURNED to the lodge, the couch was calling for a nap. But she had two things to do first.

Stephan answered on the first ring. "Hello, Stephan speaking."

She swallowed. "Hello, Stephan, this is Celeste McCarthy calling."

"Nice to hear from you, Celeste."

She took a deep breath. This was it. She wanted to feel a sense of confidence. Excitement, even. But all she could muster up was enough resolve to say what she'd called to say. "I'd like to come and visit the island," she said. "I'm strongly considering the position."

"I'm so glad to hear that, Celeste," Stephan said. "I'll have my assistant make arrangements and send you the details. Is Tuesday morning okay with you?"

"Perfect," she said. She couldn't tell if the nausea she was feeling was from her hangover or the decision she'd just made.

"We'll look forward to seeing you then."

"Likewise," she said.

"Oh, and Celeste," he said, "it's probably best not to have that type of video circulating. For your professional reputation."

"Agreed," said Celeste, her stomach sinking with embarrassment. "That...was a one-off." A one-off caused by a total disappointment.

"I'll look forward to seeing you Tuesday," said Stephan.

"Me too," she said. "See you then."

She tossed her phone onto the couch, then looked out the window and saw her parents down by the water. Perfect. They were together, with no one else around.

Celeste took the gravel path down to the waterfront, to the seasonal boathouse where they kept the canoes and kayaks. Everett was wiping down boats with a rag, while

Jeannie was organizing paddles into piles.

"Hey, sweetheart," said Everett. "Can you believe it? We don't usually take these out until June. This'll be a record for getting out on the water. Want to take one out for a spin with me?"

"Ah, no, not today," Celeste said. "But glad to see you're doing better. I hope you don't plan on lifting those on your own."

"I'll get help," he said.

"He's threatening to sleep outside tonight," Jeannie said, rolling her eyes at Celeste.

"I've been cooped up for four days. I feel like a caged animal," said Everett. "And I can't get over this weather. We've usually got a foot of snow still."

"Well, before you head out," said Celeste, "I need to talk to you both." She perched on the armrest of a Muskoka chair, then nodded toward the other seats. "Can you two take a quick break?"

"Sure thing," said Everett. He wrung out the rag he was using, wiped his hands on his pants, then sat down across from Celeste.

Jeannie sunk into the chair next to him. "I heard you put on quite a show at the brewery last night. Is Ava okay? I had half a mind to text Calista and see if there's anything going on at home." Calista was the nanny that Ava employed to help with school drop-off and pickup. She stayed with Sam until Ava got home from work and lightened Ava's load by keeping the condo tidy and doing some meal prep. Jeannie was worrying about the wrong daughter.

"What? No. Mom! You text with Calista?"

Jeannie shrugged. "What? Ava doesn't always answer her texts."

"Does Ava know that?" Celeste had to bet the answer was no. Of the four of them, Jeannie's nosiness drove Ava the most up the wall.

"Beats me," said Jeannie.

Celeste shook her head. "Ava's fine. Listen. I haven't made any decisions yet. But I want you both to know that I've been invited out to Lagoon Island on Tuesday. There's a new resort being built there, and they're interested in hiring me to manage the staff."

She studied her parents' expressions. Jeannie's eyes widened and she smiled, and Everett looked impressed. Was it genuine?

"That's great news, honey," said Jeannie, but her voice lacked enthusiasm.

"Lagoon Island," said Everett. "I was there for a wildlife-tracking seminar back in '87. It's stunning. Pretty off the grid, though, as far as I can remember."

"I know. I'm just going to check it out," said Celeste. "I haven't committed to anything."

"Well," said Jeannie, "good for you. They'd be lucky to have you."

"They sure would," said Everett. "Make sure you insist

on benefits. And a good salary. Don't sell yourself short."

"Thanks. I will," said Celeste. It was a strange feeling, telling her parents, who were also technically her employers, that she might be quitting. She hadn't expected them to beg her to stay. Likely they knew as well as she did that her tenure at the lodge was uncertain with the new owners. She hadn't expected them to be overly happy for her either; her departure would put more strain on them while they continued operations until the sale.

"All right, well, I just wanted to let you know." She stood up and motioned to the lodge. "I'm going to head in and check on things. I'll see you later on."

As soon as she was out of earshot, there would be a conversation. But that was between Jeannie and Everett. They might've been her employers but they were also her parents, and no matter what they thought of the whole thing, Celeste knew it was important to them that she felt supported.

Her heart felt a bit heavy as she walked up the path from the lake to the lodge, a path she'd walked a thousand times in her life. As a child in a bathing suit after a morning dip in the lake, Jeannie had scolding her to keep out of the way of the guests while she'd run up to grab a Popsicle. As a teenager under the moonlight, getting dropped off at the dock after a party on the island on the other side of the lake, attempting to slip in without her parents knowing she'd missed curfew.

And now as an adult, trying to make the right decision for her future, a future that felt so uncertain and so undefined. Was she making the right choice? Why couldn't there be a sign?

She had to hope that this trip would bring some clarity.

JACK WAS IN a mood.

Another last-minute cancellation had come through only hours before he was meant to meet the group, and even though they were past the point of getting their registration fee back, it still pissed him off that it was so last-minute.

In an uncharacteristic move that made him wonder if his own bad spirits were rubbing off on Bodie, the dog had chewed through one of Jack's favorite running shoes.

His kettle had shorted out that morning, so he hadn't had a coffee yet, and now he had to make an unplanned visit to Canadian Tire to pick up a new one.

The host on the local radio station was blabbering on some inane story about running out of plastic wrap. He stabbed the radio console to change the station. A sappy love song played through the speakers.

He growled and shut the damn thing off. Whoever bought into those songs was a fool, as far as he was concerned.

The Canadian Tire was on the outskirts of Sandpiper Springs, close to the lumber mill that employed many of the town's residents. He slowed his truck down as he entered the residential area.

When he passed by the run-down government-housing townhouse complex, a familiar vehicle caught his eye. You didn't see too many Hummers in these parts. As he got closer, he made out the familiar decal on the side panel. *Forrest.*

Jack scowled. He knew it. It was common knowledge that people looking for pills came around this complex, and Jack had no doubt that along with ruining his business, Forrest was still a total lowlife, either buying or selling drugs or doing them himself.

Without signaling, he pulled his truck into the gravel parking lot, blocking Forrest's Hummer in his parking spot. He was going to give the kid a piece of his mind for the second time that week. Then he was going to let the punk's dad know what his son was up to.

He got out of the truck and rapped on the driver's-side window. Forrest looked up, panic in his eyes.

"Roll down your window," Jack ordered.

Forrest opened the window a crack. "What the hell, man," he said. "Move your truck."

"Not until you admit you're still selling drugs," Jack said. "I knew it."

"You don't know anything," Forrest said. The fear in his eyes had changed to resignation. "Mind your own business."

"It is my business," Jack said. "First you open your hack operation in my territory, steal my clients. And now you're bringing that trash," he said, nodding to a gym bag on Forrest's front seat, "to a community that needs none of it. Tell me why I shouldn't call the cops right now."

"I'm not selling drugs."

"Prove it," Jack said. "Let me see what's in the bag."

"Get out of my face."

He pulled his phone from his pocket. "All right. I'm making the call."

Forest took a deep breath, then picked up the bag, opened the window the rest of the way, and shoved the bag at Jack. "I'd appreciate you keeping this to yourself," he muttered.

Jack unzipped the gym bag and stared for a second at the contents. He looked back at Forrest, who closed his eyes and leaned his head back on the headrest, then looked back at the bag in his hands, trying to make sense of what he was holding.

"Baby formula?" Jack said.

Forest opened his eyes and stared straight ahead. "Like I said. If you can keep it to yourself…"

Jack's mind raced as he struggled with what to say.

"My ex-girlfriend lives here. With our baby girl. My family doesn't know about her. I'm just trying to do the right thing by making some money to give to her that doesn't have to pass through my father."

Jack's felt his cheeks redden with shame. "Shit, man," he said. "I'm sorry." He passed the bag back through the window. It was silent for a few moments. "I won't say anything."

"Thanks," Forrest said. When he looked back at Jack, all Jack could see were the eyes of a child.

Jack turned back to his truck, then stopped, cursing himself for what he was about to do. "Hey," he said. "Meet me down at the Lemington turnpike Tuesday morning. Bring those Sage X rods. We're going to fix your cast."

For a second, he expected Forrest to rev up his engine and back up into Jack's truck, but instead, his face brightened. "Yeah? I have a new Orvis I can bring too."

Jack sighed. Could he be any more of a softie? "Yeah, bring that too," he said. "Your cast is garbage. You're telling me you've actually caught a fish before? You've got some nerve, starting your own company."

Forrest grinned. "Almost a hundred five-star reviews would say otherwise."

Jack fought off a smile as he returned to his truck. "See you in the morning, kid," he called back.

And at the end of the day, that was what Forrest was. A kid with a grown-up problem, trying his best to be a man.

HANK WAS OUT front of the tackle shop when he pulled in. "Hey, Jack," Hank said. "I heard about what went down on the river yesterday."

"Word travels fast," said Jack.

"The guys came through to the diner. Could've ended badly if you hadn't been there."

"Well, didn't," Jack said. A few hours ago, he'd have wanted to stick around for a few minutes and fill Hank in on the situation. But now he just felt sorry for Forrest.

"I'm of half a mind to call in to the licensing office," Hank said.

"Nah, no, don't do that," Jack said.

"Really? Might help clear some competition for you."

Jack knew Hank was just trying to be helpful, and he appreciated him looking out for him, but the way he said it kind of rubbed Jack the wrong way.

"All good, Hank. Leave it alone."

Hank raised an eyebrow. "You going soft on me, Wallace?"

He sure was.

"I'm going to deal with it my own way," he said. "Just don't make the call, okay? I'll see you later on."

Chapter Sixteen

THE SPEEDBOAT RIDE from Campbell River to Lagoon Island, up past Quadra Island and through the passage between the Discovery Islands, was about an hour long. Celeste had looked at a map the night before and it hadn't seemed too far away from civilization, but the trip to the remote island, where she'd already spotted seals, sea lions, and osprey, felt like a journey to another planet.

The cool air and sprays of mist off the water kept her alert as they sped through the channels between islands. Stephan's assistant had made her travel arrangements: She'd taken the early flight from Calgary to the Comox airport and would make it to Lagoon Island by noon.

For so much travel, it would be a quick visit. There would be a tour of the grounds, then a discussion about the contract over lunch in the newly completed restaurant.

She'd been up since three a.m., so Celeste was thankful that the noise of the boat's motor coupled with the wind whipping by was so loud that she wasn't forced to make conversation with the driver of the boat, a nice woman named Alexis who had been tasked with meeting her in

Campbell River and shuttling her over. Celeste's mind was spinning, and the scope of the journey she was taking was too overwhelming for small talk.

Celeste felt unsteady and untethered. She'd stood in the airport for twenty minutes, staring straight ahead and contemplating rescheduling to an early flight home and heading right back to Keystone Ridge. In the end, the fact that her stomach was growling and the only café in the Comox airport had a lineup twenty deep sealed the deal. Stephan had told her the chef was experimenting with different menu items so he'd be looking for her feedback on that as well.

The speedboat whipped across the waves, bumping forward, the scent of burning gasoline mixed with salty sea air. Celeste pulled her hood tighter around her face, trying to duck behind the boat's windshield as much as possible while also keeping the island in view. Showing up looking as polished as possible was essential, given that Stephan had witnessed her less-than-professional stage performance.

As the boat approached the inlet where the docks jutted out from the rocky shore, the resort's buildings started to come into view, mostly camouflaged by the surrounding forest. She'd read online about the mix of traditional timber cabins and luxury waterfront canvas tents that would be available seasonally, and they looked exactly like the artist's rendering.

Stephan and another man were waiting on the long dock

that jutted out from the rocks and waved as the boat's engine cut and they started to drift slowly to land.

"Here we go," Alexis said, steering the boat toward the slip Stephan was motioning her to. "Nice place here. Little remote for my liking, but that's what folks are looking for these days, I guess."

Celeste's mind flashed back to the small town of Campbell River, which wasn't much bigger than Keystone Ridge. It seemed like the woman considered it a big city compared to Lagoon Island.

"Thanks for the ride," Celeste said. She stood up, doing her best to balance herself in the wavy harbor, and accepted Alexis's hand as the woman helped to steady her.

"I'll be back at three p.m. to pick you up," she said.

"Can I text you if I end earlier?"

Alexis laughed. "Honey, you won't be texting anyone from Lagoon Island. Not for the near future at least."

She forced a laugh. "Of course," she said. "See you at three." *No texting?* Where in the hell was she?

Stephan and the other man approached, and he extended a hand to help her out of the boat. "Celeste, this is Levi Gallagher, our manager of consistency," he said.

Manager of consistency? What kind of made-up title was that?

Levi extended his hand. "Very pleased to meet you," he said. "We're so excited to show you around the property. Shall we?"

"We shall!" Celeste said, hoping no one noticed the panicked trill in her voice. She was literally in the middle of nowhere, with no cell service, and the last time she remembered seeing any other evidence of humanity had been about thirty minutes into the boat ride.

She took a deep breath. She'd made the decision to come here. And it might just be her new home.

Celeste followed Stephan and Levi to shore, taking more deep breaths while trying to focus on what Levi was saying about the shuttle boat that would be up and running by the time the resort opened, a twelve-seater something-something-name-brand-vintage-feel that Celeste knew she needed to appear excited about.

"Let's start with the cabins. I think you're going to like them."

Like was a word as understated as the Brunello Cucinelli sneakers Levi wore with his faded jeans and black blazer. An hour later, Celeste was dazzled. The resort was magical. Each of the cabins had a picture-perfect view of the water and were outfitted with the most stunning of features, all made from materials sourced from the natural landscape—cedar, sand, and slate.

The canvas tents had cast-iron stoves, heated floors, and spacious ensuite bathrooms that walked out to outdoor rain showers surrounded with rock walls, with enough of a built-out space to maintain privacy but overlook the water while showering.

The restaurant operated underneath a giant dome skylight, with a series of real trees growing throughout the dining area, making it feel as though you were sitting in the forest but in the comfort of a climate-controlled space. The trails around the property had strategically placed kiosks where guests could order fresh pressed juice or artisanal cocktails, and builders were putting the finishing touches on a spa area that featured a rock-lined glacial plunge.

It was heaven. It was refined. It was...*remote*.

"So," Celeste said, "when do you think you'll be getting service out here?"

"Oh," said Stephan. "It'll be a while before we can get a cell tower. You can hook up to Wi-Fi near the front desk, though. It's not super fast yet, but it'll be enough for operations. We're marketing this as a place to unplug."

Celeste tried not to make a face. She knew that while people might say they want to disconnect, in actuality they wanted to check in with their kids at home, post to their Instagram stories, and sneak a peek at the score of the game when their partner went to the washroom. She was about to say something but then closed her mouth. It wasn't her place. She hadn't even signed a contract yet.

Stephan checked his watch. "Shall we have some lunch?"

Lunch was served at the ocean-side restaurant, a snow-crab ceviche appetizer, saltwater lamb with zucchini and butternut squash for the main, and a black-currant soufflé with creme anglaise to round out the meal. It was swoon-worthy. If this was what the bare-bones kitchen could pull together, Celeste was dying to see what they would be putting out once they were fully staffed.

After the waiter delivered their espressos, Levi slid a thick book and a paper envelope from his satchel. He passed the book across the table first. "This is the consistency manual," Levi said as Celeste flipped through the pages. "Sort of a style guide. To ensure that a guest who experiences a Kantor Group property will be guaranteed the same experience whether they are in Tanzania, Tuscany, Tulum, and beyond."

Celeste flipped through the pages. The level of detail was astounding. Under the heading GUEST REQUESTS ADDITIONAL PILLOW there were seven steps an employee was expected to follow, starting with NOD ONCE AND SMILE PLEASANTLY and ending with WISH THE GUEST A PLEASANT AND REJUVENATING SLEEP. She almost laughed out loud when she saw that there was a section for how to ensure a guest's pet had a five-star stay.

When she looked up at Stephan and Levi, it was very clear that the policy guide was no joke. "So, this is the manual you will be using to train our staff," Levi said. "We're going through our second round of interviews now and hoping to bring the group in for training by the end of the month. That should be enough time for you to study the guide and be ready to take the others through the procedures."

"In three weeks?" Celeste said. Her mind whirled. Would that give her parents enough time to find someone to replace her? Quinn would be around to help out, but she was a little rough around the edges as far as customer service went.

Stephan nodded. "And we're hoping you'll sign today," he said. "I'm sure you can understand how we're pressed for time."

Celeste nodded. "Of course," she said, accepting the envelope Stephan passed her. He nodded encouragement for her to open it.

She slid the contract from the envelope and scanned the details. Full time. Three-month probation period. Bonus potential at the manager's discretion. Three weeks of vacation during shoulder season. The salary was comparable to what her parents paid her and included lodging.

The thought of packing up her cabin sent a wave of nausea over her. "Excuse me for a moment," Celeste said, standing up and laying her napkin on her chair. She was going to be sick.

Celeste headed to the washroom, her head spinning with possibilities. It was a beautiful resort. A secure contract with a more-than-reputable company. The other staff seemed nice enough, and the staff meals and spa discounts sounded enticing. Signing the contract was a no-brainer, wasn't it?

She didn't have a lot of time to think it through.

Instead of escaping to the washroom, Celeste slipped out of the restaurant and walked alone down the forest path that led to the back docks where the service deliveries would happen and where the staff coming and going from the mainland would disembark, so as not to ruin the more impressive sweeping ocean vista at the other side of the resort for the guests.

She walked out along the narrow wooden dock, waves lapping gently at the sandy shore underneath, her mind whirling with uncertainty.

Staring out at the water, she jumped when her phone vibrated in her pocket. Did she actually have service? She slid it out and scanned the screen, where several messages had come through, but there was only one service bar.

Quinn had texted to ask where she'd left the shed key. There was a 10-percent-off sale email from the local bakery and a message from her friend Mel in Ontario asking about visiting that summer with her new girlfriend. At the bottom of the list, there was an Instagram notification, alerting her that she'd been tagged in a post from Kassie Harris.

She went to open it, then thought for a second. No doubt it was a series of photos from the wedding, with Jack looking gorgeous and perfect in the background. She couldn't face that.

She'd half hoped he'd call after realizing what a jerk he'd been the other night at the lodge, but nothing. And now Celeste understood why. Living here, literally in the middle of nowhere, would have made a relationship impossible. He'd been right to cut things off, a realization that sent a wave of regret coursing through her veins.

Curiosity got the better of her, and when she opened the post to see a single photo—which was of her, clipboard in hand—her mouth opened in surprise. She looked closer and realized it was the moment she'd motioned to the jazz trio to start the processional song.

"What the…" she breathed. Underneath the photo, there were already over three hundred comments. Her heart pounded in her chest.

She tapped the screen and read the message that accompanied the photo.

This is Celeste McCarthy, AKA my guardian angel.

Celeste took a sharp breath in, then scrolled through the message.

When Jeff and I booked our wedding at the Butterfly Lake Lodge two years ago, we knew we'd found the right place to get married. But little did we know that Celeste would be part of the package and she would make our perfect day even more so. Gracious, warm, and creative, with a sixth sense to know what people want and need, and the patience of a saint, Celeste was an absolute gift. If you're ever so lucky as to be near Butterfly Lake, go see Celeste. She'll make your dreams come true. xoxo

A lump formed in Celeste's throat. She'd been thanked before, and a few guests had mentioned her by name on TripAdvisor. But seeing such a personal message, broadcast to millions of people—it was both terrifying and filled her up with pride and gratitude.

She looked back at the island, the trees seeming to vibrate in luscious green.

She could be that here, right? So what if there was a playbook?

"Leap of faith," she whispered, but she didn't know what that meant anymore.

Celeste slid her phone into her jacket, and her hand brushed against something in her pocket. She pulled it out to find the small kit she'd taken home from Jack's class on that first day, then opened it to find the brass hook and a few feathers and pieces of wire.

She remembered exactly what she'd said to Jack: *If I ever get stranded in the middle of nowhere, I'll know I can survive.*

A cool breeze carrying a light ocean spray moved off the ocean. Celeste slid the kit back into her pocket next to her phone.

Stephan and Levi would be wondering where she was.

She started back towards the restaurant, where their plates had been cleared away, and Stephen and Levi were eager to hear her impressions about the resort. The rest of their meeting was positive, and Celeste promised them an answer by the following day, although she'd already made up her mind.

One hour later, she was back in the boat with Alexis, wind whipping through her hair as they traveled back to the mainland.

Celeste sat back in her seat and closed her eyes, taking in slow, deep breaths of the fresh ocean air, feeling a sense of calm and resolve.

Leap of faith.

Chapter Seventeen

"That was awesome, man," Forrest said, extending his hand to shake Jack's. They'd spent the whole afternoon out on the Bow, and he was helping Forrest load his equipment into the Hummer. "Thank you."

"You're casting a whole hell of a lot better," Jack said. And he meant it. With a few tweaks, Forrest's technique had improved a lot in a short time. "Next up we're going to address that double haul. Then you might just be able to start calling yourself an angler."

"Same time tomorrow?"

"Actually, I'm heading up north for a couple days," Jack said. It had been a while since he'd been up to the cabin, and he wanted to check on how it had fared over the winter and start getting it ready for some summer visits. "But how about Saturday?"

"I'll take you out for lunch after," said Forrest.

Just before Jack was about to hop in his truck, Forrest cleared his throat. "Listen, uh, I've been thinking," he said.

Jack almost made a joke about that being a new development, but he bit his tongue. After spending a few hours with Forrest, he found himself kind of liking the kid. Given what he was going through and his openness to feedback and learning, Jack's goal now was to build him up rather than take him down. "What's on your mind?"

"My summer calendar is really booked up," Forrest said. "And I'm not ashamed to say you're a hell of a lot better at leading groups than I am." He scratched the side of his face. "What are your thoughts on teaming up? You run the tours, I'm there as a second-in-command when I can be, but most of my time I'll work on getting us bookings and manage the behind-the-scenes stuff."

Jack considered, doing his best to mask his surprise. He'd worked for years to build up his business, and he was proud of it. But there was no denying Forrest was a talented marketer, and that would free up more of Jack's time to take out groups—the part of the job he enjoyed the most. "You know, it won't take long for you to get more up to speed on all this," he said, gesturing to the river.

"I know. But it'd be a lot more fun to do this with a partner anyway," Forrest said. "Think about it at least," he added. "Maybe we can talk more on Saturday."

"I'll look forward to it," said Jack.

Teaming up. Why it hadn't occurred to him in the past was beyond him. But in the past few weeks, he'd started to see the allure of it. For his working life, but in other ways too.

USUALLY JACK LOVED the sound of raindrops on a tin roof. Today, however, the noise was grating on him. The rain was coming down in thick sheets now, and even Bodie appeared wary of going out for his morning walk. Jack threw another log into the stove, then sat back on the couch, staring out the window. He'd wanted to get up onto the roof, but it wouldn't be safe in this rain. And stocking up on firewood wasn't really an option, so he was forced inside to wait out the weather.

The book he'd brought to the cabin sat unread on the side table, and the idea of making breakfast was unappealing.

Being at the cabin was supposed to be peaceful and relaxing. But between the weather and the fact that Jack hadn't slept the night before, he was regretting his decision to come. As soon as the rain let up, he would pack up and head home. The only bright spot was what he'd resolved to do when he returned.

Bodie settled at a spot on the floor in front of him and let out a whistly sigh.

"I hear you," Jack muttered. The rain pounded even harder overhead.

He knew exactly why he'd come. Being out here in the middle of nowhere meant he had no chance of running into Celeste. Or anyone else, really. He wanted to be alone. But being alone also meant all the time in the world to be with his thoughts, which, so far, were all about Celeste. The look in her eyes when he'd told her it wasn't going to work out. The soft skin on her back that he'd traced with his hand as they'd been lying together in his bed. The playful defiance in her eyes on the river when she'd told him she wanted to do her cast *her way*.

A hundred times now he'd replayed the last time he'd seen her at the lodge and could think of a hundred different ways he wished it had played out instead of him being a selfish prick. Celeste had every right to pursue whatever job she wanted. He should have congratulated her and then waited to see how things went between them. Instead, he'd behaved even worse than he had with Christine. It had felt right in the moment. Protective. Now he was having trouble washing away the regret.

"What do you think, boy?" Jack said, and Bodie turned his head. "It's time to go see her, isn't it?"

Bodie sniffed his approval, and Jack scratched the area behind his ears. It was time. Celeste was the best thing that had happened to him in a long time, and he'd make it work long distance if he had to. Hell, he'd pack up and move out there if it meant a life with her in it.

A flash of red through the woods pulled him out of his thoughts. Bodie noticed it too and was immediately on guard. They rarely saw anyone out here.

Jack sat up and squinted, trying to make out the figure tramping through the forest, but the rain made it impossible to make out the features of whoever it was.

They'd better not be looking for shelter. Even though Jack was bored as hell, the last thing he wanted was to make small talk with a stranger who needed to get out of the rain. Maybe the hiker would pass him by.

But no such luck. The red coat moved closer to the cabin. He could pretend he wasn't there, but the smoke from the chimney was a dead giveaway. Jack sighed and stood up, ready to greet the stranger through the door.

When he swung open the wooden door, rain blew into his face, and it took him a second to realize who was standing in front of him, so soaking wet that her hiking jacket and pants stuck to her slight frame, and it was clear that her cheeks weren't just wet with rain.

"Holy hell, Celeste," he said. She looked up at him and let out a small sob, then wiped her face with the soaking wet sleeve of her jacket. Her skin was red, and she was shivering.

He opened his mouth to speak again but was too surprised. He made way for her to enter the cabin, then shut the door behind them. She stood in the small entranceway, a puddle forming at her feet.

"Here," he said, making a move to help her take off her jacket. "Let me take that. I'll get you something dry to wear. Come over by the fire."

She allowed him to help her strip down to the leggings and sweater she was wearing under her hiking gear. He grabbed a thick blanket from the couch and pulled it around her shoulders. "What the hell are you doing coming all the way out here? In this weather? How did you even find the place?"

She sniffled a little. "I needed to see you," she said. "I remember you telling me about the painted rock and the marked path."

"You put yourself in a lot of danger," Jack said, his heart melting with the thought that Celeste, who avoided the outdoors in even the best of conditions, had braved the elements to get to him. At the same time he felt furious with her for hiking on her own through unknown woods. "Never mind that now," he said as her body convulsed again in shivers. "Come here."

She allowed him to pull her into his arms, his hands rubbing her arms over the blanket to generate heat. He looked down to see her eyes closed against his chest and drank in the feeling of her. It took everything inside of him to pull himself away. "Your clothes are damp," he said. "You're never going to warm up."

He left her standing beside the fireplace, then dug into his duffel bag and pulled out a crewneck sweatshirt and a pair of fleece-lined hiking pants that she'd be swimming in, but they had a drawstring waist. He passed her the clothes. "I'm going to go boil some water," he said. "I'll be back in a couple of minutes."

"Thanks," she said.

He returned with a mug of hot black tea to find her sitting on the floor in front of the fireplace, Bodie lying on his back across her lap, happily accepting the tummy scratches Celeste was giving him.

"What an opportunist," Jack said. He joined her on the floor and passed her the mug.

"He's like a fur blanket," said Celeste. She smiled, then nodded toward the table, where his unused place setting from breakfast was waiting to be used. "Cloth napkin? What's happened to you?"

Jack grinned. He'd thrown the napkin into his duffel at the last minute. He'd come to like using it, and it was less wasteful than paper. "I could ask you the same," he said. "I can't believe you made that hike on your own. A few weeks from now, there's a chance you could run into a grizzly on that trail. Did you tell anyone where you were going?"

"I left a note," she said. "I didn't want anyone trying to stop me. Or worse, trying to join me." She took a sip of the tea. "I've had a lot of…attention recently."

"What do you mean?"

"I guess you don't follow Keystone Konnection."

He tried to maintain a neutral expression but was certain she could detect a hint enough of amusement. "Well, that was some video," Jack said. "Didn't know you could dance like that."

She shook her head. "I'm over the embarrassment. But Ava brought me out that night because I was incredibly upset about what happened between us. Because the truth is, Jack, that I've fallen for you. And all I wanted was for you to be happy for me and for us to talk about some way we could move forward, even though things might be a little messy. Because you and I—" Celeste paused, steadying her breath as the words tumbled out. "You and I might work really well together. But you just left, so I have no idea if you feel the same way."

Jack was quiet. He watched her shoulders rise and fall under his old sweatshirt, then fixed his gaze on the forest outside of the window. He knew what he wanted to say; he just wanted to be sure it was the right thing.

Celeste broke the silence. "I didn't take the job on Lagoon Island."

He turned to face her. "But you were so excited about that job," he said, his voice deep with concern. "They were rolling out the red carpet for you."

"It's an incredible place. And it was a good job...on paper. But to be honest, I was mostly excited about the certainty that the offer gave me. It wasn't the job I was really into—I just wanted the sure thing. And..." She gulped, clearly trying to hold back tears. "I'm trying my best to believe what you told me—that I've got what it takes to survive whatever happens. I've decided to believe that everything's going to work out with the lodge, which is where I belong. If it doesn't, then I'll find something else. But I don't want to give up on what I really want before I know it's a done deal." She reached over and took Jack's hand in hers. "That's why I'm here. I hope you're not done with me."

Jack pulled Celeste closer, kissing the top of her head. "I was wrong to bolt like that," he said. He kept her close against him, feeling the rise and fall of her chest as she breathed, waiting for him to explain himself. "It was stupid of me. You have every right to pursue whatever goal you want. And I made it all about me and stuff I clearly never moved on for. The truth is I would have packed up and moved anywhere for you. I just didn't know if that's what you wanted."

"It is."

Jack took a long, steadying breath. Celeste had just said the exact words he'd been wanting to hear, and knowing that she felt that kind of devotion to him gave him a sense of reassurance he'd never felt before, like he was standing on the most solid ground. "Okay," he said, his warm, firm grip on her hand tightening even further.

He looked up to find her eyes searching his. "So, you're staying," he said.

Celeste nodded. "I heard there's a part two to this really great class I just took, and I thought I'd better give it a go."

Jack couldn't stop the wide smile spreading across his face. He leaned over and slid his arms around Celeste, pulling her slightly up and off the carpet so that her legs crossed over his lap. "Well, I don't know. You didn't technically complete part one. Are you ready for the challenge?" He leaned in and kissed the soft, sensitive skin on her neck.

"I've heard the teacher has very high standards," she whispered.

"Oh, he does," Jack said. "I don't think I'm going to be teaching anymore, though," he said. "Something else has come up since I last saw you."

"That underwear-modeling gig came through?"

"Not yet. Still waiting for the right contract."

"So, what is it?"

"Well, it's really too soon to tell." Even saying it out loud felt a bit crazy, but he had a good feeling and wanted to trust it. "I might have found another match, in an unexpected place." He filled Celeste in on what had happened with Forrest, how they'd spent the morning out together on the river and how Forrest had actually been a humble and gracious student, even if his jokes were kind of stupid. How Forrest had surprised Jack by floating the idea of teaming up.

"I like the sound of that," Celeste said.

It was unexpected. And there was only one surprise bigger than that, and she was wrapped up in his arms. "So, what do you think—you like it out here?" he asked.

She glanced around the cabin. "I mean…it could use a woman's touch."

He kissed her again. "You can touch whatever you want," he said, pulling her in even closer, unable to believe he'd almost let her go.

Celeste laughed. "But wait," she said. "I haven't told you

what helped me make my decision." He watched as she stood up and pulled her jacket off the rack by the fire and rustled through her pocket, then returned to the floor beside him. "Someone taught me about things that endure. Because they work."

Jack kissed her softly. "If that's the only thing you learned from that class, I'll still call it a success."

The End